Kate Fortune's Journal Entry

It's so difficult to stand by and watch my loved ones get hurt. Poor Allie. Her beauty has always brought her so much attention. And now an obsessed fan is after her. It breaks my heart. Luckily, I can count on bodyguard Rafe Stone to take good care of my granddaughter.

Allie's not used to men loving her for herself. And Rafe's own scars prevent him from believing in love. Now I hope the music box I left her will help them both realize the power of inner beauty. Though the box is chipp~~ed~~ ~~on the~~ ~~ugh~~ outside, it st~~...~~

In the meant~~ime~~ ~~...~~ investigate wh~~...~~ ~~...~~ my family. Because I suspect this crazed stalker is after more than just my granddaughter....

A LETTER FROM THE AUTHOR

Dear Reader,

I hope you enjoy reading *Beauty and the Bodyguard* as much as I enjoyed writing it. I got *so* caught up in the continuing saga of the Fortune family—aren't they a fascinating, dynamic group? They certainly put the Carringtons and the Ewings in the shade!

I particularly liked writing Allie and Rafe's story. She's so strong, yet so vulnerable. She has to be in her profession. For all its glitz and glamour, modeling is one tough business. As I learned during my preparation work for this book, being a professional model takes discipline, patience, an ability to absorb endless criticism and, above all, a sense of humor. Allie certainly possesses these qualities, plus a few distinctive ones all her own. Rafe is just my kind of guy, too. A man who's sure he's seen it all—until he goes head-to-head with a certain determined female and discovers there are still a few surprises left in store for him.

Happy reading!

Merline Lovelace

Beauty
and the
Bodyguard

MERLINE LOVELACE

Silhouette Books

Published by Silhouette Books

America's Publisher of Contemporary Romance

To Marcy and Mike…thanks for
making our return to New Mexico such a
wonderful adventure of fun and friendship.

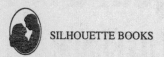 SILHOUETTE BOOKS

BEAUTY AND THE BODYGUARD

Copyright © 1996 by Harlequin Books S.A.

ISBN 0-373-50179-X

Special thanks and acknowledgment is given to Merline Lovelace
for her contribution to the Fortune's Children series.

MERLINE LOVELACE,

as a career air force officer, served tours of duty in Vietnam, at the Pentagon and at bases all over the world. During her years in uniform, she met and married her own handsome hero and stored up enough exciting tales to keep her fingers flying over the keyboard for years to come. When not glued to the computer, she goes antiquing with her husband, Al, or chases little white balls around the golf courses of Oklahoma.

Merline loves to read and write sizzling contemporary stories and sweeping historical sagas. Look for her next book, *Halloween Honeymoon,* coming from Silhouette Desire in October. She enjoys hearing from readers and can be reached at P.O. Box 892717, Oklahoma City, OK, 73189.

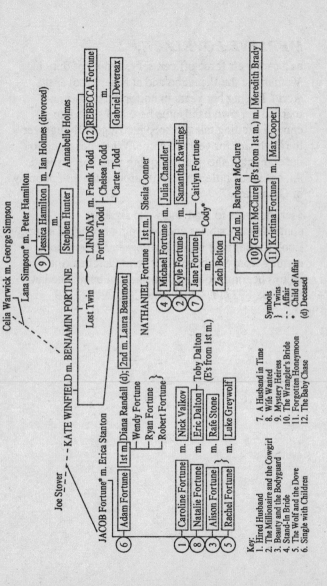

Celia Warwick m. George Simpson

Lana Simpson* m. Peter Hamilton

(9) Jessica Hamilton m. Ian Holmes (divorced)

Annabelle Holmes

Stephen Hunter

Joe Stover

--- KATE WINFIELD m. BENJAMIN FORTUNE

LINDSAY m. Frank Todd | Chelsea Todd
Fortune Todd | Carter Todd

(12) REBECCA Fortune m. Gabriel Devereax

Lost Twin

NATHANIEL Fortune | 1st m. | Sheila Conner

(4) Michael Fortune m. Julia Chandler

(2) Kyle Fortune m. Samantha Rawlings — Cody*

Caitlyn Fortune

(7) Jane Fortune m. Zach Bolton

2nd m. Barbara McClure

(10) Grant McClure (B's from 1st m.) m. Meredith Brady

(11) Kristina Fortune m. Max Cooper

JACOB FORTUNE* m. Erica Stanton

Adam Fortune | 1st m. | Diana Randall (d); 2nd m. Laura Beaumont

Wendy Fortune
Ryan Fortune } Toby Dalton
Robert Fortune (E's from 1st m.)

(6) Adam Fortune

(1) Caroline Fortune m. Nick Valkov

(8) Natalie Fortune m. Eric Dalton

(3) Alison Fortune m. Rafe Stone

(5) Rachel Fortune m. Luke Greywolf

Symbols
} Twins
-- Affair
* Child of Affair
(d) Deceased

Key:
1. Hired Husband
2. The Millionaire and the Cowgirl
3. Beauty and the Bodyguard
4. Stand-In Bride
5. The Wolf and the Dove
6. Single with Children
7. A Husband in Time
8. Wife Wanted
9. Mystery Heiress
10. The Wrangler's Bride
11. Forgotten Honeymoon
12. The Baby Chase

FORTUNE'S Children

Meet the Fortunes—three generations of a family with a legacy of wealth, influence and power. As they unite to face an unknown enemy, shocking family secrets are revealed...and passionate new romances are ignited.

ALLIE FORTUNE: This cover girl had learned that most men were after two things: her money and her body. Rafe Stone *seemed* different, but the sexy bodyguard was getting paid well to protect her. Could she truly trust him?

RAFE STONE: The ex-mercenary had been hired to keep Allie out of trouble, not in it! But trouble was what she'd find if she kept tantalizing him with her potent combination of beauty and brains!

KATE FORTUNE: The Fortune clan still thinks their beloved matriarch is gone, but Kate is secretly close by...watching over them. Not even her own "demise" can keep her from sharing the moments of her family's lives.

MICHAEL FORTUNE: "Better dead than wed" had always been this high-powered executive's motto. Could Kate's bequest of a ruby ring persuade him to see what—and *who!*—is right under his nose?

LIZ JONES— CELEBRITY GOSSIP

Are the Fortunes *doomed?*

As if they haven't had enough disasters befall them, now glamorous Allie Fortune, the new Fortune Cosmetics spokesmodel, has a crazed fan stalking her. Lucky for her she's got that hunky bodyguard to protect her *assets!*

Kate's recent death has brought about a massive reorganization within the Fortune empire, causing the stock values to plummet. And another mysterious break-in at the lab has caused further setbacks in the creation of some secret formula. Word has it, if this formula doesn't get developed, the company will go bankrupt.

Just between you and me, I *personally* wouldn't invest a dime in that sinking ship!

So, is this a professional or a highly personal vendetta against the Fortunes? Only time will tell. But if you're like me, you'll want to stick around for this ongoing saga.

One

She noticed his tie first.

Having spent ten of her twenty-five years as a model, Allie Fortune had seen every extreme of fashion. During her career, she'd glided down runways wearing items from collections the most generous critic could only describe as eclectic.

This particular piece of neckwear went well beyond eclectic, however, and got lost somewhere on the other side of atrocious. Red and orange fish-eyes splashed against a purple background made a fashion statement Allie couldn't begin to interpret.

Wondering what kind of man would combine such an outrageous tie with conservative black slacks, a pale blue cotton shirt and a cream-colored linen sport coat that stretched at the seams of his impressive shoulders, Allie raised her eyes to his face.

She'd never met him before. She would have remembered him if she had. He stood out, even among the diverse crowd of advertising executives, art directors, photographers, chemists and production engineers gathered at the party her older sister had thrown for the people involved in launching Fortune Cosmetics's new line. Under his neatly trimmed midnight hair, his face was lean and tanned and striking, despite the scars on his chin and neck...or perhaps because of them. Certainly she would have remembered his eyes. Silvery blue and framed by black lashes a good number of her friends would have committed serious mayhem for, they riveted hers across the crowded room.

For several long seconds, those cool blue eyes held her pinned. To Allie's considerable surprise, his scrutiny sent a spine-tingling tension arcing through her. The tiny hairs at her nape lifted, as though stirred by an unseen breeze. A sort of prickly awareness drifted across her shoulders and down her back, left bare by the plunge of her dress. For a moment, the excited buzz of conversation about Fortune Cosmetics's new product line seemed to lose its sharp-edged focus.

Being watched wasn't a particularly unique experience for a woman who'd spent most of her adult life under the harsh, unforgiving eyes of makeup artists and stylists and photographers. Yet an inexplicable little shiver shimmied along Allie's nerves as the awareness intensified. With the ease of long practice, she maintained an unruffled poise as she returned his stare.

Then, slowly, deliberately, his gaze traveled from the top of her upswept hair, down the soft lines of her lemon-colored chiffon tank dress to the tips of her open-toed sandals. When his gaze snared hers again, she felt a small jolt of surprise.

Allison Fortune had learned to expect a wide range of reactions in men's eyes when they looked at her. Cool dismissal wasn't usually one of them. Her interest piqued, she took a small sip from the crystal champagne flute she held in one hand.

"Would you like another glass?"

The deep, slightly slurred voice at her side pulled her attention from the dark-haired stranger across the room. "No, thank you, Dean. I'm fine."

Dean Hansen's blond brows slanted into a frown. "You've been nursing that glass for over an hour. It's probably flat by now."

"I've got to watch my calories," she returned lightly. "I'm leaving for a shoot tomorrow, remember?"

Her escort's scowl deepened, marring the lines of his handsome, classically Scandinavian features. "I remember. God, Allie, you just flew in from New York this morning. When are you going to spend a little time in Minneapolis? More to the point, when the hell are you going to spend some time with me?"

His voice rose querulously, carrying over the hum of conversation and the jazzy beat of the trio at the far end of the high-ceilinged living room. Several heads turned, and Allie caught sight of her older sister's face, sharp-set with worry. As chief of marketing for the vast array of products produced by Fortune Cosmetics, Caroline Fortune Valkov shouldered a heavy responsibility. Since their grandmother's death in a plane crash six months ago, those responsibilities had become almost unbearable burdens.

Although their father, Jake, had stepped in and taken over full control of the corporation at Kate Fortune's death, he'd had to reorganize and streamline several subsidiary companies to keep the huge conglomerate afloat while the lawyers sorted through Kate's financial affairs. As a result, stock values had nosedived. To make matters worse, a series of break-ins and a fire at their main chemical lab had caused several severe setbacks in the development of the new line of products Allie would help launch.

They'd staked so much on this new line, her father and Caroline and every other member of the Fortune family. Even without the secret "youth" formula her grandmother had been working on when she died, this collection of new beauty products would buy them time to pull the corporation out of its financial slump. Thousands of people worldwide depended on Fortune Cosmetics for their livelihoods. There hadn't been a layoff in Kate's lifetime. Jake was grimly determined that he wouldn't be the first Fortune to send their workers to the unemployment lines.

Which was why Allie had put her budding acting career on hold and agreed to be the "face" for the new line. Why she hadn't told anyone but her twin the precise details about the frightening phone calls she'd received. And why, with those sharp lines in Caroline's forehead, she didn't need Dean Hansen causing a scene at her sister's party.

Allie studied the man she'd been dating off and on for several months. Dean's flushed face told her this would be the last function she'd attend with him. The brimming tumbler of Scotch in his hand also told her he wouldn't take his marching orders well. Deciding it was only fair to him to settle things between them before she left for New Mexico tomorrow, she set her champagne flute on a sofa table.

"Why don't we go out on the terrace?" she suggested, nodding toward the bank of French doors lining one wall. With any luck, the breeze from the lake would counter the effects of his Scotch.

Dean's frown disappeared. Amber liquid sloshed as he set his drink down beside her. "Lead the way, beautiful."

Allie wound through the noisy crowd and stepped through the open doors. Crossing the wide terrace, she leaned both hands on the low stone balustrade and dragged in a deep, welcome breath of the August night. After two weeks of meetings and consultations with advertising executives in New York City's sweltering mugginess, the Minnesota air felt unbelievably clean against her skin.

Dean's uneven tread echoed on the flagstones behind her, almost lost in the rise and fall of laughter and music from inside. His big hand curled around her arm.

"Let's get away from the noise. Walk down to the lake with me."

Nodding, Allie slipped off her sandals and left them on the terrace. When she stepped off the stone stairs, her toes curled into the dewy grass. She'd run barefoot through these lush lawns with her twin sister so many times during the summers they stayed with their grandmother. She and Rocky had chased fireflies and giggled and shared their girlish dreams with Kate. Now Kate was dead, and Allie had put her dreams on hold.

With Dean beside her, she made her way down to the lake. The long, sloping lawn muted the sounds of the party. Gradually the noise died to a faint murmur. For a few moments, she heard only the lapping of indigo water against grassy banks and the cheerful chirp of cicadas. Then Dean's hoarse voice disturbed the harmony of the night.

"God, Allie, you're so beautiful." Sliding a hand behind her neck, he turned her to face him.

"You're not so bad yourself," she replied, "but..."

His thumb pressed her lips. "No buts. Not tonight. Not when you're leaving in the morning."

When he tried to pull her forward, Allie placed her palms against his chest. "We need to talk, Dean."

"We'll talk later."

To her surprise, he dug his fingers into the back of her neck and dragged her forward. Frowning, she stiffened her arms.

"Dean, please!"

"Dammit, Allie, don't do that! Don't freeze up on me again."

"You've had too much to drink," she said evenly. "Let me go."

"Not this time," he growled, his breath hot and smoky with Scotch. "I've been dancing to your tune for months now. Every time I try to get close, you poker up or turn away. What's with you, Allie? What kind of game are you playing with me?"

"I don't play games, with you or anyone else."

"The hell you don't. What else would you call it when you put on that beautiful come-hither face, then pull back every time I try to touch you?"

Wedging her arms against his chest, Allie fought to keep her voice steady. Although she'd inherited a fair share of her grandmother's fire, along with her hair, she'd long ago learned to hide her own emotions behind the smiling facade the public wanted to see.

"I've told you repeatedly. I like you...as a friend. I enjoy your company...as an escort. But I'm not going to go to bed with you."

"Why not?"

He sounded so aggrieved, so much like a sulky teen denied the use of the family car, that she had to smile. "Because I don't want to, Dean."

As soon as the words were out, Allie recognized their truth. Her smile slipped a little.

The sad fact was, she hadn't wanted to in a long time. Too long. With Dean or anyone else. Not since she'd discovered that men in general, and her former fiancé in particular, were far more taken with Allison Fortune's face and money than with Allison Fortune herself. That rather humbling experience hadn't totally turned her off either sex or men. She just hadn't yet found a man who could see past her glamorous public image to the private woman within.

Dean Hansen was a case in point. Instead of accepting her blunt admission that she wasn't looking for an affair when they first met, he'd taken it as a personal challenge. Every time she flew home to visit her family and agreed to dinner or a movie with him, he'd tried to tease and flatter her into having sex with him. Now, apparently, he'd run out of flattery.

His mouth twisting, he used his hold on her neck to drag her face a few inches from his own. "You don't want to, huh? Maybe I should make you want to."

"Maybe you shouldn't. Let me go, Dean."

"I don't think so. Not this time."

"Yes." She ground out the word. "This time!"

He wasn't expecting the sharp elbow jab to his stomach. His breath whooshed out, and his hold slackened enough for Allie to wrench free. She stepped back a few paces, holding on to her temper by a thread.

"Get out of here," she told him coldly. "Don't come back to the party. You're no longer welcome."

She turned to head back to the house. When his hand wrapped around her upper arm again, Allie's temper slipped its tight reins. Whirling, she planted both palms against his chest and shoved.

Taken by surprise, Hansen stumbled backward, his arms windmilling wildly. Too late, Allie saw that the combination of Scotch and his own momentum was going to take him into the lake. In his inebriated condition, the fool would probably drown.

"Oh, for—!" She jumped forward, grabbing for his jacket lapels. "Dean, watch out!"

Frantically he snatched at her. His hand snagged one of the thin straps holding up her tank dress. The strap dug into her shoulder, then snapped. With a comical look of surprise on his face and a swatch of lemon chiffon clutched in one fist, Dean splashed into the lake.

His uncoordinated entry sent a wave of cold water splashing over Allie. Moments later, his clumsy, cursing exit added considerably to her drenched state. By the time she'd helped him clamber back onto the grassy bank, her irritation had given way to the sense of the ridiculous that helped her through long, exhausting shoots, when everything that could possibly go wrong did. Biting her lower lip to contain her smile, she held her soggy dress up with one hand while Dean tried to swipe thick, oozing mud off his face and hands.

Her escort didn't appear to share her humor at the situation. Cursing, he shook his hands to fling off the mud, then advanced on her, his blond hair straggling down his forehead. In the pale moonlight, his eyes glittered with fury.

"You little..."

"I'd suggest you take a hike before you end up in the lake again. This time permanently."

The deep, drawling voice spun both Dean and Allie around. Peering through the darkness, she spotted a shadowy figure lounging against a tall, silver-barked river oak.

Shoving his wet hair out of his eyes, Dean glared at the shadowy figure. "Who the hell—?"

"You've got about ten seconds to get out of here, pal."

"Look, *pal*..."

"Yes?"

The combination of polite inquiry and deadly menace in the single syllable made Allie blink and Dean's cheeks puff up like a blowfish. Indignant but more wary now, he tried to bluster it out.

"This is a private conversation."

Levering his shoulders away from the trunk, the intruder strolled into the wash of moonlight. Allie drew in a quick breath as she identified the gaudy collage of red and orange and purple.

"According to the lady, the conversation's over," the stranger offered casually. "I make it about five seconds now."

"Who is this character, Allie?"

Since she had no idea, she ignored the question. "I think you should leave, Dean. Now."

His jaw worked for a few seconds. Then the stranger sauntered forward, with a coiled, controlled economy of movement that sent the bigger man back a pace.

"Fine," Dean snarled. "I'm leaving. It's time I found a real woman to spend my time with instead of a plastic-faced doll, anyway."

Neither Allie nor the man beside her said a word as Hansen stalked off, his shoes squishing lake water at each step. With his departure, the summer night settled around them like a cloak. Only this time, Allie wasn't conscious of the wavelets lapping against the banks or the chirping cicadas. This time, the man before her absorbed her entire attention.

His eyes a pale silver in the moonlight, he surveyed her with the same dispassionate objectivity he'd displayed earlier. Once more, he measured her from head to toe, only this time his gaze lingered on parts in between.

Belatedly Allie realized that her gauzy tank dress was plastered to her like a second skin. Since Dean had taken a good chunk of its bodice into the lake with him, she could only hope that her bikini panties and scrap of a bra concealed more than they revealed. She was sure the cool breeze had puckered her nipples, along with the rest of her flesh, into giant goose bumps.

At the thought of this enigmatic stranger's eyes on her breasts, Allie's fingers scrunched on the torn chiffon. For the second time that night, an unfamiliar sensation rippled through her. Not quite attraction. Not exactly curiosity. More an awareness that crept through her at some subconscious level and left her feeling off balance.

With some effort, she controlled an instinctive feminine impulse to cross her arms over her breasts. She hadn't felt this self-conscious about her body since she'd posed for the college classmate who'd begged her for some test shots to add to his portfolio. Those shots had launched both Dominic's career and her own, and Allie had shed her prudish modesty under the unforgiving eye of the camera. Or so she'd thought.

When his gaze finally made it back to her face, his eyes held a predatory male gleam that Allie recognized instantly. A slow, liquid disappointment spilled through her.

Earlier, this man's cool detachment had intrigued her almost as much as his tie. For a few moments, she'd imagined he was different. That he didn't care about appearances. She'd actually let herself believe he was trying to see past the image she projected to the person within when he pinned her with that cool look.

He wasn't detached now, if that brief flare of masculine interest was any indication. Telling herself she was crazy to be disappointed because a man appreciated the exterior packaging she worked so hard to perfect, Allie lifted her chin.

"I don't think we've met before."

"No, we haven't."

When he didn't appear inclined to elaborate, she extended her free hand. "I'm—"

"I know who you are, Miss Fortune."

Her hand dropped slowly. The fact that this stranger knew her name didn't particularly surprise her. Mass marketing and the explosion of media interest in the lives of top models had made them into the superstars of the nineties. As a result, Allie's face usually garnered instant recognition whenever she walked into a room.

Lately, it had garnered something else, as well. Something dark and frightening.

An echo of the call that had dragged Allie from sleep only last night whispered through her mind. She bit her lip as her inexplicable preoccupation with the man standing before her slipped, like a car skidding on a patch of ice, then skidded into unease. Silently she stared up at him.

Etched by moonlight, his face showed no softness, only sharp, uncompromising angles. A square chin, darkened by late-night shadow. A nose that had collided with some solid object once or twice in its past. Lean cheeks. And those scars on the left side of his chin and neck...

Swallowing to clear a suddenly dry throat, Allie broke the little silence. "Well, you may know me, but I don't know you. Who *are* you, and what are you doing here?"

"My name's Rafe Stone. I'm your bodyguard, Miss Fortune."

Stunned, Allie stared up at him. "My what?"

"Your prospective bodyguard," he corrected. "I've been asked to take on the job of guarding your person."

"By... by whom?"

"By your father."

For several long moments, Allie could only gape at him. Then anger washed through her. Swift, hot anger that she refused to let this stranger see.

Jake Fortune couldn't stop trying to control her, any more than he could his other children or his wife or his thousands of employees. On the heels of that bitter thought came the cynical realization that her father was just trying to protect the "face" that he'd staked his company's future on.

"When did my father hire you?"

"We haven't closed the deal, but the understanding was I'd start tonight, if I decided to accept the job."

"Tonight?" She lifted a scornful brow. "Then why didn't you intercede a little earlier, Mr. Stone? You must have seen me struggling with Hansen."

"I haven't negotiated the terms of my contract with your father yet. Besides," he added, his gaze drifting to the wet fabric bunched in her hand, "for a while there, I wasn't any surer than your overmuscled Viking friend just what kind of game you were playing."

Allie stiffened. "Then I'd say you're not very perceptive, for a man who makes his living watching people."

One dark brow lifted sardonically. "Perceptive enough to see who invited whom for a stroll in the dark."

"You know, Mr. Stone," Allie replied, spacing each word carefully, "I don't think I particularly want you guarding my person."

"Maybe you should talk to your father about it."

"I will."

She tried for a dignified exit, which wasn't easy, with her French twist scraggling down her neck and her dress clinging to her thighs with every step. The walk up to the house seemed to take several lifetimes longer than the walk down to the lake.

Rafe followed at a more leisurely pace, his eyes on the slender figure ahead of him. He wondered if she had any idea of the way that wet handkerchief of a dress clung to her body, or what it did to his lungs. Rafe grimaced at the thought. Of course she did. Women like Allison Fortune were probably born knowing their impact on men.

All right, so her wide-spaced eyes, full mouth and endless limbs were the stuff of late-night fantasies. So he'd felt an immediate, gut-level urge to stroke his thumb across those impossible cheekbones when he first spotted her across the noisy room. Rafe possessed what he assumed was a normal testosterone level. Any man's hands would itch to touch her skin, just to see if it was smooth and creamy as it looked.

Unfortunately, his initial reaction to Allison Fortune had been mild compared to the one Rafe experienced now. Watching her stride up the sloping lawn with an easy, long-legged grace detonated small implosions of heat, one right after another, just below his belt line. For all her almost boyish slenderness, the woman had a figure that would stop traffic on any street, in any city, on any continent.

Good thing she didn't want him guarding that body, Rafe thought cynically, any more than he wanted the job. He didn't need the staggering sum Jake Fortune had offered, nor did he need the kind of complications his involuntary reaction to Allison Fortune could cause. The reputation he'd earned in certain circles for his ability to penetrate seemingly impossible locations and extract hostages brought him more business than he could handle. He'd succeeded in that dark and dangerous world because of his ruthless ability to focus on his target. If he let himself get involved with the person behind that target, he'd lose the razor edge of concentration his work demanded.

Besides, Rafe had survived one disastrous experience with a beautiful woman, and he was a man who learned from his mistakes. His ex-wife wasn't anywhere near Allie Fortune's class in looks, of course, but her breathless baby-doll beauty had turned more than a few heads.

Phyllis had left him three years ago, when it became clear that no amount of surgery would erase the scars left by the bomb that had almost killed him and his client. Rafe had made it a point to steer clear of any entanglements ever since…which made him all the more wary of his instant animal attraction to the woman in front of him. With each step, his resolve to tell Jake Fortune to find another man hardened.

Among other things.

She reached the stairs that led to the terrace, and Rafe wondered idly if she intended to march into the brightly lit living room with her every curve on display. Probably. According to the dossier he'd had compiled on Allison Fortune, there weren't many parts of her that hadn't been captured in explicit detail on film and displayed to the eager public. Despite her huffy little speech to Eric the Blonde a few moments ago, this woman had made a career of playing games. When she draped herself across a rock on some mist-swept shore, as she had in a full-page ad that had made Rafe break out in a cold sweat, she was trying for an effect. The ad might make the female half of the population want to run out and buy the tiny scrap of fabric the manufacturers called a bathing suit. The male half, Rafe among them, fantasized about sliding the straps down her arms and . . .

She halted abruptly, with one foot on the first stone step. Worrying her bottom lip with her teeth, she glanced up at the open French doors, then turned to Rafe.

"Would you go inside and find my father? Ask him to meet me in the library in fifteen minutes."

Rafe had never been real good at taking orders, even during his years with Special Forces. In this instance, though, he was as anxious as Allie Fortune to terminate their association before it officially began.

"Yes, ma'am," he drawled with exaggerated politeness.

Her eyes narrowed. "Are you this sarcastic with all your prospective clients?"

Silently acknowledging that he wanted to be a whole lot more than sarcastic with this particular prospective client, Rafe shook his head. How the hell could a simple collection of flesh and bone stir such atavistic male urges in him? He hadn't felt this powerful an attraction for any woman since Phyllis. Hell, he hadn't felt it *for* Phyllis.

"No, Miss Fortune. I'm not."

Before she could respond to that one, he started up the broad stairs. His footsteps rang on the flagstones as he headed into the house, determined to tell Jake Fortune he wasn't interested in the job.

TWO

Rafe soon discovered that Jake Fortune didn't take no for an answer. For all his aristocratic airs, the man had the instincts of a street fighter. Tall, silver-haired, and impeccable in a gray Armani suit, he leaned his hips against the leather-topped desk that dominated the library, crossed his arms and cut right to the bottom line.

"I'll double your retainer fee."

Rafe regarded his would-be employer thoughtfully. He knew the value of his services, and felt no compunction about charging his clients according to their ability to pay. That Jake Fortune would double his initial offer without a qualm told Rafe there was more to this particular job than the client had admitted.

There always was, he thought cynically. He had the scars to prove it. Still, he didn't need the money, and he sure as hell didn't need to fan the small, hot flames Allie Fortune lit in him.

"It isn't a matter of money," he told her father. "My specialty is extraction under hostile conditions, not baby-sitting."

Both men turned at the sound of a small laugh. A willowy blonde stood framed in a side door.

"It's usually a matter of money where my husband is concerned, Mr. Stone."

Annoyance flickered across Jake Fortune's face before he wiped it clean of all expression. "In this instance, at least, you're right. Come in, Erica. Perhaps you'll be more successful than I've been in convincing Mr. Stone to provide Allie protection."

When Erica Fortune walked into the oak-paneled room, Rafe detected traces of the daughter in the mother's elegant carriage and cool, controlled grace. But the older woman's stunning beauty seemed fragile, almost brittle.

The dossier on Allison Fortune included several pages about her parents, as well. A former beauty queen and the first model for Fortune Cosmetics, Erica Fortune had enjoyed what the media painted as a fairy-tale marriage to the founder's son. Judging by the tension she brought into the library with her, Rafe wouldn't have put a lot of credence in the happily-ever-after part. Whatever was causing the obvious stress between Erica Fortune and her husband, however, she put it aside in her daughter's interest. Her green eyes softened as she pleaded with Rafe.

"Please reconsider, Mr. Stone. I don't know how much my husband told you about these calls my daughter has received, but they worry us."

"He mentioned that a fan got hold of her unlisted number and made some highly erotic remarks."

"Erotic?" Erica sniffed. "They're obscene. The man's a pervert."

"Until the police track him down, I agree it's wise to provide your daughter with security, Mrs. Fortune. I just don't think I'm the right man for the job."

"Why not?"

Rafe tugged at his tie. He couldn't exactly tell this woman that he didn't want to spend two weeks with her daughter because she generated a few highly erotic thoughts in him, too.

"Look, Mrs. Fortune..."

"Erica, please."

"Erica. I..."

A sharp rap on the massive double doors that led to the main hallway cut off Rafe's reply. When Allison Fortune swept in a moment later, she cut off his air supply, as well. Irritated anew by her impact on him, Rafe stopped fiddling with his tie and shoved his hands in his pockets.

She was punctual, he had to give her that. True to her word, she'd taken less than fifteen minutes to change into a silky-looking pair of turquoise pajamas with one of those little Chinese collars and fancy embroidery. If her makeup had been disturbed by her dousing from the Nordic type she'd been stringing along down by the lake, she'd repaired it quickly enough. She looked untouched, and eminently untouchable.

Her glance flicked over Rafe, then settled on the older woman. A small frown marred the smooth perfection of her forehead. "I thought this bodyguard business was Jake's idea. Did you know about it, too, Mother?''

Interesting, Rafe thought. She referred to her father by name, but not her mother.

''He told me about it when Mr. Stone showed up at the party tonight,'' Erica replied.

''Oh? Well, he neglected to tell me.''

As his daughter turned to face him, Jake Fortune's patrician features took on a hard edge. ''You're always so adamant about preserving your privacy, Allie. I knew you might object to having someone with you twenty-four hours a day. I thought it best not to discuss the matter with you until I ascertained Mr. Stone's availability and finalized our arrangements.''

''You were right. I do object to Mr. Stone's presence twenty-four hours a day. So you can unfinalize your arrangements.''

Rafe thought about setting them both straight. He hadn't agreed to any arrangements, final or otherwise. But neither Fortune seemed particularly interested in his input at that moment.

''I'd like you to think about this. You know how important you are to—''

''Yes, I know. To Fortune Cosmetics.''

Jake's mouth thinned. ''I was going to say, how important you are to the entire family. I don't like the idea of some obsessed fan worrying you and disrupting your life.''

''Or the shoot,'' she added softly. Her tobacco-brown eyes held her father's for a long moment.

His jaw tight, Jake Fortune turned to his wife. "You talk to her. Evidently I can't anymore."

Brushing past her husband, Erica moved to her daughter's side. "Please be sensible, darling. This campaign is so important, not only to Fortune Cosmetics, but to your career."

"I'm starting a new career after this campaign, remember?"

"I know, I know. And you're wise to think about acting as a full-time career. Modeling is a brutal business, where a woman's worth is measured only by her looks." Erica's musical voice took on a bitter edge. "Unfortunately, that's true in more than just modeling."

She didn't turn her head, didn't so much as glance at her husband, but Jake Fortune stiffened. If his wife noticed his reaction, she ignored it.

"But you're just reaching your peak, Allie. You've got years ahead of you yet."

"Mother..."

"You're more photogenic than I ever was, and you've agreed to launch the new line. If it's as successful as we hope, you'll reach the highest plateau in your career. I just wish we had decided on a studio shoot for this campaign, instead of a natural setting," Erica continued, her voice sharp with worry. "I don't like the idea of you all alone for two weeks, out in the middle of nowhere."

The corners of Allie's full mouth edged upward. "Come on, Mother," she teased gently. "A five-star resort a few miles outside Santa Fe is hardly the middle of nowhere. And you know as well as I the size of the team necessary for this shoot. I'll hardly be alone.''

Later, Rafe would tell himself that he would have walked out of the library as planned, if it hadn't been for the hint of laughter in her voice. And for that damned almost-smile. It softened the lines of her face. Added a gleam to her eyes. Hit him somewhere in the vicinity of his left kidney.

The half smile hooked him, but a different emotion altogether reeled him in a few moments later.

Erica's huge square-cut emerald flashed as she reached for her daughter's hand. ''But that disgusting person said he'd find a way to come to you, and prove how much he loved you.''

He'd said a lot more than that, Rafe guessed instantly, or Allie wouldn't look away to hide the flicker of emotion that darkened her eyes. Rafe had been in the business long enough to recognize fear, no matter how well or how quickly hidden.

Dammit, he thought in disgust, why couldn't she have remained just a beautiful face? Why did he have to catch a glimpse of a vulnerable, frightened woman behind that sophisticated facade? Allison Fortune he would have walked away from without a qualm. The woman who refused to let her family see her fear tugged at his professional instincts. He couldn't help wondering what else she was hiding behind that glamorous front.

Okay, he rationalized, he could do this. He'd trained himself not to become emotionally involved with his clients. He could spend two weeks with Allison Fortune, shield her from this kook who got off by whispering obscenities over the phone, and pocket the outrageous fee her father offered. Assuming, of course, the lady agreed to protection... and to playing this particular game by his rules.

"Please, darling," Erica pleaded, her voice breaking a little. "It's bad enough we didn't even know about this disgusting pervert until the police called here, asking to speak to you. Don't make it worse by refusing our protection until they track him down."

With a small sigh, Allie patted her mother's hand. "I'm sorry. I should have told you about the calls. I just didn't want to worry you. Or the rest of the family," she added after a slight pause. "You've all had enough problems since Kate died."

"Then you'll agree to additional security?" Jake asked.

She slanted her father a cool glance, then turned those incredible eyes on Rafe. Strange, he'd never realized how changeable a color brown was before. In the space of a heartbeat, it could vary from deep, rich mocha to a flat, uninviting mud.

"I agree," she said after a moment. "But with certain conditions."

"I don't operate with restrictions."

"And I can't operate without a certain regimen," she returned. "I run every morning, and during a shoot I have to get at least eight hours of sleep a night. All I'm asking is that you structure your security procedures around my schedule, if possible.''

Rafe hadn't seen the inside of a gym in years, and he'd never been much for jogging, but he figured he could keep his client covered during her morning jaunts. As for those eight hours a night in bed . . .

With some effort, he banished the combustible image of Allie Fortune all doe-eyed and sleep-soft. Telling himself he was ten kinds of a fool, Rafe agreed. Reluctantly.

''I think we can accommodate your schedule.''

She hesitated, obviously as unenthusiastic as he was about the next two weeks. ''Then I'll leave you to negotiate the terms of your contract with my father. If you decide to accept the job, I'll meet you at the airport. We have a ten-o'clock flight to Santa Fe.''

''Well, I'm glad that's settled,'' Erica said with a sigh of relief as her daughter brushed a kiss across her cheek and started for the door.

''Not quite,'' Rafe drawled.

Allie paused with one hand on the doorknob.

''If I'm going to be responsible for your safety, Miss Fortune, I have a couple of conditions of my own.''

''Such as?''

''Such as no more strolls down to the lake—or anywhere else—unless I go along as a chaperon.''

After so many years in front of the camera, hiding her thoughts had become almost second nature to Allie. Her job was to project the emotions the photographer and art director wanted, not her own feelings. So she kept her expression carefully neutral while she debated whether to tell Rafe Stone to take a flying leap in the lake—or anywhere else.

As much as she wanted to put this man in his place, however, Allie had to admit the idea of a bodyguard had some merit. Although she routinely exercised basic security precautions against the weirdos who regularly fell in love with faces in magazines, these late-night calls had become too personal, too disturbing. She didn't want this crazy to continue disrupting her life. Even more to the point, she didn't want him to disrupt this shoot. Her older sister, her parents, her entire family, had staked everything on this campaign. Their tightly planned schedule allowed for minimal slippage.

Despite his brusque manner, or perhaps because of it, this Rafe Stone had routed Dean Hansen easily enough. He certainly looked as though he could take care of one obnoxious, if obsessive, fan. Besides, she'd only need his protection for two weeks. Three at most. Just while they were on location. The police had assured her the security at her New York condo was adequate. She could dispense with his services when they returned to the city for the final studio work.

Two weeks. She could put up with Rafe Stone's constant presence for two weeks and still maintain the inner equilibrium.

Maybe.

"What's your second condition?" she asked.

"If I perceive a threat to your safety, you follow my orders. All of them. Immediately. Without question."

Allie wasn't stupid. Nor was she foolhardy. In the event of a real threat, she'd be more than happy to let this man handle it.

"Agreed."

Her acquiescence didn't appear to afford him a great deal of pleasure. "I'll pick you up at nine and take you to the airport," he said brusquely.

"No further negotiations with my father, Mr. Stone?"

"No. And the name's Rafe."

She hesitated, then extended her hand. "I go by Allie."

Her touch was warm and smooth and altogether too electric. Rafe curled his fingers around hers for the required few seconds. When she slid her hand out of his, her heat tingled against his palm, and he felt the damnedest urge to make a fist and trap it.

Two weeks, he told himself grimly. He'd spent almost that long on his belly in the dust, staking out a supposed terrorist hideout in southern Spain. If he could handle that band of inept would-be revolutionaries, he could handle himself around Allie Fortune.

Maybe.

By eight-thirty the next morning, Allie was having second, third and fourth thoughts. She'd spent a restless night, trying without notable success to adjust to the idea of Rafe Stone's disturbing presence in her life. Her sleeplessness hadn't been helped by her sister's acid observation that she'd let Jake do it to her— again.

"Why didn't you stand up to him?" Rocky asked, picking up the refrain she'd left off last night only when Allie threatened to tie a pillowcase over her head. Perched comfortably on a window seat in the bedroom the girls had shared since childhood, Rocky went after her twin with the piranha-like ruthlessness of a loving sister.

"You should have told Jake to stuff it when he pressed you to do this campaign. You know how burnt out you are. You've been trying to stuff acting lessons in between your runway shows and advertising shoots. You only have time for an occasional date with jerks like Hansen. And now you've got this creep calling you in the middle of the night. What you need, sister mine, is a hot and fast and furious affair."

"Right."

"I'm serious. You need someone to make you kick back and enjoy life again. Preferably a man who doesn't worship at the altar of your beauty."

"What I need is for you to get off my back," Allie retorted, tossing a nightshirt into her weekender.

"Me, or Jake?"

"Both of you."

"So tell him!"

"I'm not you, Rocky. I don't make an art form out of challenging people."

"Bull-loney! Don't pull that innocent act on me. You never hesitated to challenge anyone when we were younger. You just did it so sweetly, no one but Kate ever saw through your angelic facade. It's just since her death that you've let Jake and Caroline and the whole family take over your life."

Allie gripped her zippered makeup bag in both hands as a now familiar pain lanced through her. Involuntarily her gaze drifted to the battered tin carousel sitting on the dresser.

Kate had seen her granddaughters' wide-eyed fascination when she'd first acquired the carousel. Laughing, she'd given the German-made toy to the girls to play with, even though it was an expensive antique. As Kate was so fond of saying, there was nothing more precious in the world than a child's joy. The tomboyish Rocky had soon tired of the little merry-go-round, but Allie had delighted in its filigreed canopy and prancing horses throughout her childhood. Now dented and dinged from years of use, the tin carousel was Allie's most cherished reminder of her grandmother. Kate had left it to her in her will as a personal keepsake.

Dropping the makeup bag, Allie walked over to the dresser. Unerringly, her fingers wound the key just the right number of times. Too many, and the melody tripped and hurried, like a twittering sparrow chasing another bird away from its nest. Too few, and it slowed to a sluggish crawl.

She released the key, and a Chopin polonaise tinkled through the air. One after another, the miniature horses dipped and rose, pawing the air in time to the music.

As the music wound down, Rocky sighed. "God, I miss her."

Allie swallowed to ease her aching throat. "Me too."

Pulling her nightshirt out of the suitcase, she wrapped it carefully around the little carousel, then tucked the bundle in amid her underwear.

"That's why I didn't tell Jake to stuff it," Allie told her sister slowly. "And why I'm going to New Mexico. Kate spent her life building Fortune Cosmetics. If I can help keep it from falling apart, I will."

"All right," Rocky conceded, rising. "Have it your way. But I wish you'd let me fly you to Santa Fe. I'd feel better about the whole situation if I had a chance to shake out this goon Jake's hired and see what he's made of."

Allie shuddered. "The idea of you shaking us out is exactly why I don't want you to fly us to New Mexico. The last time you took me up in one of Kate's planes, I lost the contents of my purse, my camera bag and my stomach. At least a commercial charter doesn't do wheelies."

A pained expression crossed Rocky's face. "Bicycles do wheelies, Allison. Skateboards do wheelies. Twin-engine Piper Comanches do three-point reverse spins, of which that was a perfect example."

"Whatever it was, I'm not anxious to repeat the experience." Allie zipped her weekender shut, then glanced at the bedside clock. "If you want to check Rafe out, you can come downstairs. He's picking me up in ten minutes."

"Rafe?"

"The goon," Allie replied dryly.

A speculative gleam entered Rocky's eyes. "Hmm . . . Maybe this bodyguard business isn't such a bad idea after all. Two weeks. Just you and him."

"And a crew of forty or so."

Rocky dismissed the crew with a wave of one hand. "Whatever. I definitely have to check the guy out."

"Come on, then. He should be here any moment, and I don't want to keep him waiting."

Her twin sketched her a salute. "Yes, ma'am! Right away, ma'am!"

Thirty minutes later, Allie's leather sole was tapping the polished vestibule floor. Rocky had temporarily deserted her, gone to the kitchen in search of a cup of coffee. She had only her growing irritation for company while she waited for her bodyguard.

Pushing back the sleeve of her pink gabardine tunic, Allie flicked another glance at her watch. Normally, she handled delays with more patience. They were inevitable in her profession. Photographers always seemed to need a different lens. Props mysteriously disappeared just when they were needed. But Rafe's tardiness only added to her burgeoning doubts about their tentative arrangement. So much for his promises to accommodate himself to her schedule.

When the chimes sounded a few moments later, she opened the door, wincing a bit as splashes of fire-hydrant red, carroty orange and violent purple filled her vision. Last night, Rafe's tie had intrigued her. In the bright light of day, it assaulted her senses.

"Good morning," she offered in a clipped tone, reaching for her bag. "We'd better hurry. We're late. The others will be waiting."

Rafe's jaw tightened imperceptibly. After three years, he should be used to the reaction his appearance caused. But Allie's involuntary flinch and curt greeting came on top of a near-sleepless night and several long hours on the phone this morning, nailing down the status of the investigation into her calls. Rafe didn't like being late, any more than he liked the information he'd finally pulled out of the New York Police Department. Consequently, his greeting was as terse as hers.

"They'll have to wait a little longer. You need to change. You're too conspicuous."

Surprised, she glanced down at her outfit.

Rafe didn't have any problem with her black slacks, but the hot-pink tunic with the black braid looped under one arm and the military trim in glittering jet would catch any man's eye, especially with Allie wearing it.

"I'll share one of the tips of the trade with you," he told her. "Unless you're baiting a trap, you do your best to disguise the prey."

Rafe could see that she didn't particularly like hearing herself described as prey. But after listening to the transcription she'd given the police of her late-night calls, he couldn't describe her as anything else.

"For the next few weeks, at least," he continued, "you need to remain as inconspicuous as possible."

Thick, shining hair brushed her shoulder as she tilted her head, studying his face. Rafe braced himself as her gaze drifted to his neck.

"It might be easier for me to remain inconspicuous if my bodyguard didn't wear red and orange fish-eyes," she suggested.

Rafe fingered his tie, wondering for a moment if he'd misread Allie's reaction when she opened the door. He'd barely restrained a wince himself when he first saw the item in question. But it had been a gift from the five-year-old he'd rescued from an enclave of vicious, heavily armed white supremacists. The girl had been kidnapped by her father, who didn't believe that the courts or his ex-wife held any authority over him. Jody had picked out the tie herself, she'd told Rafe solemnly. He'd worn it then to please her, but the thing had since become a sort of personal talisman. In this instance, at least, it served a useful purpose.

"I'd rather people's eyes were drawn to me than to you," he told his client. "The tie helps, almost as much as the scars."

Her eyes widened slightly at his reference to his disfigurement. Rafe had learned that most people preferred to tiptoe around the subject, if they mentioned it at all. He'd never learned to tiptoe.

"You can do your part by dressing a little less like a..." He raked her with a quick glance. "Like a supermodel."

Rafe half expected a pout or a protest. In his admittedly limited experience, the last thing a beautiful woman wanted was to downplay her attractions. To his surprise, she curbed her obvious impatience at the delay and motioned him inside.

"I didn't bring much with me from New York, but I can borrow some jeans or something from Rocky."

Rafe turned the name over in his mind as he stepped inside. Rocky. Rachel Fortune. Allison's twin sister.

"Do you want a cup of coffee or something while I change?"

"No thanks."

"I'll just be a moment."

Shoving his hands in his pockets, Rafe leaned a shoulder against the wall and made a leisurely inspection of the entry hall and the huge living room beyond. Last night, the house had overflowed with noise and people. Rafe had noted its elegance, but absorbed little of its character.

This morning, sunlight streamed through the fan-shaped window above the door and warmed the oak flooring to a golden glow. Fresh flowers added bright spots of color to the greens and blues of the high-backed chairs and overstuffed sofas grouped around the living room. For all its vastness, the Fortune mansion gave the impression of a home.

Rafe certainly couldn't have said the same for the apartment he'd moved into in Miami after his divorce. Although it was furnished with all the basics, it lacked some indefinable homelike quality. Maybe that was due to the fact that he spent only a few days a month there, if that. For a moment, Rafe toyed with the idea of coming home to a place imbued with beauty and quiet elegance...and to a woman with the same qualities. A woman like Allie.

He shook his head at the errant thought. He'd been down that road once. He wasn't about to travel it again. The sound of footsteps echoing against the oak floor banished his unpleasant memories, and Rafe straightened as Allie walked into view.

His first thought was that he'd done some stupid things in his life. Having his client exchange her loose slacks for well-washed denims that hugged her hips and showed off the tight curve of her bottom ranked right up there among the dumbest. Every male past puberty would trip over his tongue when she walked by.

His second was that she'd changed more than her clothes. At first, Rafe couldn't pinpoint exactly what. Her sorrel hair swept her shoulders in the same thick wave. Sooty lashes framed the same chocolate-brown eyes. Her full mouth looked as tempting as it had when she opened the door to him a few moments ago.

But something about the way she held herself triggered an instinctive, gut-level question in Rafe's mind.

It took a few seconds before he realized that the woman returning his stare wasn't Allie.

Christ! The dossier had indicated that she and her sister were identical twins, but that brief annotation didn't begin to describe their astounding similarity. If Rafe hadn't spent half the night imprinting his client's features and mannerisms on his mind, he might never have known this wasn't her.

Their differences, he decided objectively, were more a matter of style than of appearance. Unlike Allison's classic sophistication, Rachel opted for a more rugged look. She wore a brown leather aviator jacket with the sleeves pushed up, a white knit top, boots, and the jeans that had made Rafe's heart skip a few beats. He could only hope they wouldn't hug Allie's slender figure as faithfully as they did her sister's.

"You must be Rocky," he said slowly.

Grinning, she nodded. "Right. And you, I sincerely hope, are the hired gun."

Before he could respond to that, Allie walked back into the vestibule. Rafe saw instantly that his hopes had been in vain. In glove-soft jeans, a cream-colored turtleneck and a misty blue tweed jacket, Allison Fortune looked like every man's dream of a very bright, very sexy campus coed.

The only way he could make her inconspicuous, Rafe decided grimly, was to wrap her in a blanket from head to toe.

He dug a small, specially designed beeper out of his pocket. "Here, clip this on, and make sure you keep it within reach at all times."

Frowning, she turned the little black box over in her hand. "What is it?"

"It's a tracking device and emergency signal."

"How does it work? I don't see any button to push."

"There isn't any button. If you need me, just grip the unit in your hand and squeeze. The pressure and heat from your palm will set off a pulsing signal on my unit."

She fumbled with the tight clip.

"The rest of the time, the device emits a continuous signal keyed to a special frequency that only my unit can pick up."

Her hands stilling, she glanced up. "Continuous?"

"So I can track you anytime, night or day."

"I've heard these devices were available," Rocky put in. "The military developed them initially. Now people buy them to keep track of their dogs," she added, grinning at her sister.

A look of distaste crossed Allie's face. "I'm not sure I like the idea of being on a leash, like someone's toy poodle."

"It's part of the security package."

Rafe's brusque tone said clearly that she could take the entire package or leave it. Allie didn't miss the unspoken message. Her mouth tightening, she lifted the clip and jammed the unit onto the inner pocket.

"Let's go," she said shortly. "We're late."

Twenty minutes later, Rafe pulled off the airport access road and drove up to the private hangar Allie indicated. She'd told him some of the site crew would be traveling with them on the small chartered jet. She hadn't bothered to mention that half the population of Minneapolis would be turning out to see her off.

He stepped out of the rental car, tensing as a figure darted out of the milling crowd and dashed toward them. Rafe relaxed only marginally when he saw that it was a teenage girl.

"Hi, Allie! We heard you were leaving this morning. Will you sign my T-shirt?"

Before Rafe could put himself between his client and the girl, the passenger door slammed and Allie walked forward. "Sure. Got a pen?"

"I got some new test shots for my portfolio," another long-legged, coltish girl said shyly as she joined them. "Would you look at them?"

Within moments, Allie was surrounded by a clutch of tall, gangly young women. Wannabes, Rafe presumed, all pressing her for tips or advice or autographs. The rest of the crowd appeared to consist primarily of men in coveralls with logos from various airlines on their pockets. They watched the proceedings with avid interest. Occasionally one would nudge another in the ribs and share a comment that resulted in a lewd grin.

Rafe's jaw tightened at their expressions, but Allie seemed impervious to the reactions she caused among her male admirers. Smiling and answering the girls' peppered questions, she made her way toward the hangar. The men fell back to let her pass. As she reached the side door, Rafe turned to scan the crowd for the representative of the rental agency he'd arranged to pick up his car.

At that moment, Allie gave a little squeak.

Rafe spun back around just as an arm looped around her neck and dragged her through the door.

Three

Rafe crashed through the hangar door and launched himself at Allie's attacker.

Seconds later, she was pushing herself up off the floor, gasping. Her assailant lay facedown on the concrete, with one arm twisted up between his shoulder blades and Rafe's knee planted squarely in his back. When he sputtered an obscenity and tried to dislodge the crushing weight that held him pinned, Rafe shoved his arm up higher.

"Ow!" His shout bounced off the high hangar ceilings.

"Break his other arm, if you like, but not that one. He can't shoot left-handed."

The low, husky voice penetrated Rafe's pounding, adrenaline-charged consciousness at the same instant as Allie's breathless protest.

"Rafe! That's...Dominic. The photographer!"

The man's nose scraped concrete as he turned his head toward the sound of her voice. Only then did Rafe notice his hair. Or the lack of it. The left side of his scalp was buzz-shaved to a glistening white. The right sported long, flowing black locks. The effect was every bit as startling this morning as it had been when

Rafe first saw the man, last night at the party. He loosened his grip on the man's wrist, but took his time unplanting his knee.

"Get him . . . off me!"

"Rafe, please! This is Dominic Avendez. He's my photographer."

When the man finally regained his feet, he rubbed his wrist and glared at his attacker. Rafe knew the exact instant the photographer noted the scars. His gaze snagged at chin level, and he swallowed visibly. Turning to Allie, he demanded an explanation.

"Who *is* this character?"

"He's . . ."

"The name's Stone," Rafe replied deliberately. "Rafe Stone. I'm Miss Fortune's bodyguard."

"Bodyguard? Since when does she need a bodyguard?"

Flashing Rafe a silent warning, Allie stepped forward. "It was Jake's idea, Dom. With so much riding on this ad campaign, he wanted a little extra insurance."

"Insurance? Hell, the whole shoot almost went down the tubes because of him."

"Are you okay?"

"No." Scowling, he rotated his aching shoulder.

Allie moved to his side. "Come on, let's get you to the plane."

In what Rafe now guessed was a habitual gesture, the man started to loop his good arm around Allie's neck. He caught himself just in time and threw her bodyguard a wary glance. His scowl deepened at the expression on Rafe's face, but he tucked his arm through Allie's, instead of wrapping it around her neck.

Rafe stood still for a moment, watching the un-likely pair walk toward the small, sleek jet parked just outside the open bay doors at the far end of the han-gar. Allie towered over the stocky photographer by half a head, and her luxuriant reddish brown mane formed a stark contrast to his long/short, black/white hair style. But it was obvious they were good friends. *Very* good friends. Her face held genuine sympathy and an unmistakable affection as she soothed the man's ruffled feathers.

So why hadn't she told Avendez about the calls? Rafe wondered. Why didn't she want her...friend...to know the real reason behind the sudden appearance of a bodyguard in her life, any more than she'd wanted her parents to see her fear last night?

Not for the first time, it occurred to Rafe that Allie Fortune hid a good part of herself behind the face she showed to the public. Wondering at the woman be-hind the mask, Rafe bent to pick up the duffel bag he'd dropped when he launched himself through the air.

A throaty chuckle brought his head around. A short, stocky woman with cropped brown hair grinned up at him.

"The last time Dom's face scraped the ground, he had a camera angled up Allie's skirt. That shot did more for the panty hose industry than any ad campaign in its history. I'm Xola, by the way. Dom's stylist. I do the drops and props.''

Rafe took the hand she held out, not surprised at its firm grip. She might stand a good ten inches shorter than his own six foot one, but she exuded a down-to-earth, no-nonsense air that contrasted with the startling sensuality of her voice.

"Welcome to the team, Rafe."

"Thanks." He flicked a glance at the semiscalped photographer climbing into the plane. "I think."

Xola's laughter flowed over him like melted chocolate, rich and dark and deep. "Don't worry about Dominic. Allie will coax him out of his sulks eventually. She always does. Come on, we'd better load up, or we'll get left behind. If you haven't already noticed, Allie's a stickler about keeping on schedule."

"I've noticed," he drawled. "Tell them I'll be right there. I just have to find the rep from the rental-car agency."

Rafe strode toward the hangar door, making a mental note to have background checks run on the entire crew, particularly one Dominic Avendez.

By the time they arrived at Rancho Tremayo, the sprawling old hacienda a few miles north of Santa Fe where the rest of the crew had already assembled, Rafe had discovered that his client was a stickler about a number of things in addition to punctuality.

Her diet figured right up there near the top of the list. Throughout the long flight, she politely had refused the snacks the others offered. Since Rafe hadn't had either the time or the foresight to lay in supplies for the trip, he'd gratefully dug into Xola's cache of Snickers, unsalted cashews and grapefruit juice. By late afternoon, his stomach had been rumbling with increasing frequency and resonance.

As he and Allie followed the resort manager through the walled adobe compound to the guest houses, the tantalizing scent of beef cooking in a spicy sauce that filled the air added to his growing discomfort. The hacienda had been converted into a world-class resort, he'd discovered, and its main restaurant had won a coveted Excellent rating from *Gourmand* magazine. Rafe was all set to settle Allie in her quarters and explore the validity of the culinary rating when he ran smack up against another one of his client's sticking points—her tendency to modify the rules of the game to suit her own preferences.

Her luxurious, beam-ceilinged casita enchanted her. Smiling, she complimented the effusive manager on the striking Navajo blanket hanging above the fireplace and the combination of pale pink adobe walls and mauve floor tiles shot with turquoise.

The manager stuttered something about soothing desert jewel tones and ushered her through an arched doorway to the bedroom. Rafe guessed he still hadn't quite recovered from the combined effect of Allie's stunning long-legged beauty, Dominic's half head of hair and Xola's spine-shivering, rippling laughter.

While the too-tanned, too-attentive manager and Allie chatted, Rafe did a quick security sweep of the three rooms. The bedroom's windows were set high in the walls, he noted with satisfaction, and fixed with sturdy locks. The only other entrance to the casita was through a side door in the kitchenette, which could be bolted from within. That left the main door opening onto the sitting room. It had a peephole and locks any ten-year-old with a plastic library card could get through in a few seconds flat.

"I want a locksmith out here within an hour to install a dead bolt," he told the manager. "We'll need two keys for it. I'll keep one, and Miss Fortune the other."

The man brushed a hand over his styled hair. "But... But the housekeeping staff will need to get in. And Maintenance..."

"Miss Fortune will call when she's ready for housekeeping. You can contact me if Maintenance needs access."

The manager looked to Allie for confirmation. She hesitated, then endorsed Rafe's orders with a nod. "You'd better have the locksmith make three keys, though. Dominic will need one."

Rafe refused to acknowledge the feeling that spiked through him. It wasn't any of his business who his client chose to spend her time with, as long as she did so under certain controlled conditions. He didn't consider Avendez much of an improvement over the Viking, but he didn't think Allie would appreciate his opinion on the matter.

"Two keys," he countered. "I won't be responsible for your safety if I can't control access."

Her mouth thinned. "I don't think you understand. Dom and I will be working late most nights, reviewing the day's production and the next day's schedule."

"Fine. You can let him in, or I will. You agreed to play this by my rules, remember?"

For a moment, Rafe thought she would argue. The smooth skin of one cheek twitched, and a spark of anger or resentment darkened her eyes. It was gone before he could decide which it was. When she turned to face the manager, the cool facade she showed to the public was back in place.

"Two keys," she said stiffly.

"My casita is right next to yours," Rafe told her. "Number eight. I'm going to dump my gear, then go to the office to go over the guest lists. After that, I need to check the physical layout of the resort." And scarf down some food. "I'll be back for you in an hour. Use the beeper if you need me before that."

With a supreme exercise of will, Allie refrained from slamming the door behind the two men.

Damn Stone! With his beepers and his keys and his controlled access, he was making her feel caged. Or like a dog in obedience training. Tossing her purse onto the bed, Allie yanked at the zipper on her case.

By the time she'd put away her clothes, she'd calmed enough to realize how counterproductive her anger was. She hadn't even begun the stressful part of her job, and already she was wound tighter than a steel spring. If she was going to make it through the next few weeks, she'd have to shrug off Rafe's abrupt manner, just as she did Dom's mood swings and Xola's exacting demands.

She could do this. She was a professional. So was Rafe. He was just doing his job, as she had to do hers. She just needed to call on the reservoir of patience she'd stored up all these years in front of the camera. Pretend he wasn't there, as she did the crew that hovered around her during a shoot.

Not four hours later, Allie had reached the bitter conclusion that she couldn't share the same planet with Rafe, let alone the same general vicinity, and maintain the inner tranquillity needed for her work.

She didn't understand how one man could invade her space and her consciousness so completely. It wasn't that he put himself forward or was the least bit intrusive. On the contrary, when he escorted Allie to dinner at the resort's restaurant, he chose a table for himself at the periphery of the noisy crew, who welcomed her into their midst. But she'd noticed the startled glances he drew, and Xola's friendly smile when she joined him for coffee. Allie had been conscious of him all through dinner, and now, when she should be concentrating on her work, she felt his presence in every pore.

He sprawled with loose-limbed grace on the sofa, one foot propped on the edge of the rough-planked coffee table as he skimmed with astonishing speed through a paperback. Slanting him a sideways glance, Allie studied him with a model's keen insight for line and form. He'd shed his awful tie, opened the neck of his dark blue cotton shirt and rolled up his sleeves to reveal strong, muscular forearms. The gleaming highlights in his dark hair made a startling contrast to the rugged, tanned planes of his face and...

"Are you interested in this new production-scheduling technique or not?"

Allie slewed her attention back to the man seated in the chair beside hers. "Of course I am."

Dom stabbed at the keyboard of the notebook computer he'd set on the table between them. Within seconds, a colorful flowchart was painted across the screen.

"Pay attention," he ordered irritably. "I get big bucks to teach this at RIT, you know."

"I know," Allie said soothingly.

In his more generous moments, she knew, Dom would acknowledge her own contribution to his spectacular career. His earlier shots of Allie had helped him break into the tough, competitive world of fashion photography. Their later work together had solidified his international reputation and led to an appointment as a guest lecturer at the Rochester Institute of Technology, a center of excellence for photographic arts and sciences since George Eastman had rented a factory loft there in 1880.

In his crankier moods, though, Dom tended to forget their long association, as well as his manners and his maturity. Unfortunately, he'd remained cranky since Rafe had slammed him into the concrete earlier this morning. Despite Allie's best efforts to coax him into a better mood, he'd been terse and uncommunicative all day. When he showed up at her casita after dinner for their usual preview of the next day's schedule, she'd hoped his enthusiasm for his work would restore his good humor. It hadn't.

A moment later, she winced as Dom slammed down the lid on his computer.

"I can't concentrate," he announced, tucking the notebook under his arm. "I'm going to drive into town and check out the sites we'll be using for the shoots."

Halfway to the door, he stopped and issued an ungracious invitation. "Want to come? With your watchdog's permission, of course."

"No, thanks," she replied easily, too used to Dom's sarcasm to let it bother her. "If you want to start shooting by seven, I'll have to be in makeup by six. Which means..."

"I know, I know. You have to be up at five for your run. So go to bed and get some sleep, or even I won't be able to disguise the lines in you face. You're not getting any younger, you know," he added with a touch of malice.

Laughing, Allie crossed the tile floor and planted a kiss on the bald half of his head. "Between your camera and your computer and your creative imaging techniques, you can disguise anything. You're a genius, Dom. A thoroughly obnoxious genius, but I love you."

The photographer shot Rafe a fierce look, then deliberately hooked an arm around her neck. "Yeah, well, I can tolerate you. On occasion."

Allie accepted his kiss, then closed the door behind him and twisted the key in the shiny new dead bolt. She turned to find Rafe's dark eyes fixed on her. The relief she'd felt at her friend's brief spurt of good humor vanished instantly.

For the life of her, Allie couldn't understand why this man should affect her so. She'd spent the past ten years enduring the intense scrutiny of a host of men and women who ruthlessly dissected the most minute details of her face and figure. Since she'd catapulted to the top of her profession, she'd learned to deflect the curious, sometimes avid, stares of her fans. Yet, from the first moment she found Rafe watching her at the party, Allie hadn't been able to shake the sensations he generated in her.

What did he see when he looked at her through those steel-blue eyes? she wondered.

Just what everyone else saw, the practical corner of her mind said mockingly. A face. Two arms. A body that would have been considered bony and unattractive in the pre-Twiggy days, though a good number of men today seemed to find it sexy. Including, Allie remembered, the late-night caller who'd brought Rafe into her life in the first place. Despite her best efforts to control it, a little shiver rippled down her arms.

"Cold?"

His deep voice piled another set of goose bumps on top of the first. Grateful for his excuse, Allie rubbed her arms.

"A little. It's going to take me a few days to get used to Santa Fe's chilly nights."

"And to its altitude. You might want to rethink this early-morning jog."

"I rethink it every morning," she admitted wryly. "Once when the alarm goes off, and again when I finally drag myself out of bed."

He linked his hands behind his head. "But you still jog every morning?"

With some effort, Allie kept her gaze from sliding down the washboard of his ribs to the flat plane of his stomach. For heaven's sake, she'd seen more male torsos than she could count during her career. Just because this particular male radiated a lean, coiled power that she'd seen demonstrated to startling effect in the hangar this morning, that was no reason for her pulse to skip every other beat.

"I use diet and exercise to control my weight, instead of drugs," she replied with a credible show of nonchalance. "I've watched too many of my friends destroy their careers and their lives by substituting chemicals for food."

He flicked a quick glance at the door. "You have some interesting friends."

"Yes, I do," she replied evenly. "And despite his ups and downs, Dom's one of the best."

He made no answer to that, and a small silence settled over the room. Allie searched for something to say, but everything that came to mind seemed inane, or far too personal. Somehow, she couldn't bring herself to ask about his friends. Or how he'd gotten into the business of guarding bodies. Or how he'd acquired those scars. Yet she found herself intensely curious about his past. With a slight shock, she realized she knew next to nothing about the man who'd invaded her life so completely in the past twenty-four hours. Still, she valued her own privacy too much to intrude on his.

"I think I'll call it a night."

He rose and snagged a sleeveless sheepskin-lined vest from the chair where he'd tossed it. Shrugging into it, he tucked the paperback into a pocket and closed the small distance between them.

"Five o'clock, huh?"

"Five o'clock," she returned firmly, trying to ignore the tingling sensation his proximity generated. "It's the first day of the shoot. We have to stick to the schedule, or Dominic will tear out the rest of his hair."

"Is that what happened to it? He pulled it out?"

She should open the door, Allie told herself. Or take a step or two away and put some distance between them before she turned and answered his question. For reasons she would have to examine later, in the privacy of her room, she didn't do either of those things. Instead, she leaned back against the door and studied him through her lashes.

From this angle, she couldn't see his scars. Only his strong, square chin, stubbled with a late shadow. And his mouth, a few inches from hers. And eyes more silver than blue. What did they see? she asked herself again, wishing she didn't know the answer. Wishing she didn't see it in the male intensity of his gaze.

He saw a face. Nothing more. And so much less.

"Actually," she replied, in answer to his question, "his doctor shaved it off. Dom got impatient during one of our shoots...."

Rafe's snort told her he'd already figured out that wasn't an unfrequent occurrence.

"Instead of waiting for a ladder, he climbed a tree to get a better angle. Unfortunately, the tree was loaded with poison oak. Some tangled in his hair, and the result... Well, it wasn't pretty for a long while."

"I wouldn't call it pretty now."

"You would if you'd seen him six months ago," she retorted.

"I don't think so." Lifting his hand, he brushed a careless knuckle down her cheek. "This is what I'd call pretty."

The touch seemed to surprise him as much as it did Allie. Frowning, he dropped his hand at the same instant she jerked her head back.

"Sorry," he said tightly. "That was out of line."

As surprised by his apology as she'd been by the unexpected caress, Allie struggled to match his quick recovery. "Apology accepted."

She stepped aside, and he reached for the door handle. "Lock the door behind me."

"I will."

"And keep the beeper handy."

"I will."

"Good night."

"Good night."

His mouth twisted in disgust, Rafe pulled the door shut behind him and listened for the snick of the lock. He couldn't believe he'd given in to the insane impulse to touch her. She was his client, for God's sake. And the kind of woman he had no business touching.

Except... Rafe wasn't quite as sure now that he knew *what* kind of woman Allison Fortune was. Every time he thought he had her pegged, she threw him another curve.

Hunching his shoulders against the chill, he walked the arching adobe corridor that led to his casita. With each ring of his boots on the Spanish tile, his mental composite of Allie Fortune shifted focus a bit.

He almost believed her line about Avendez. Even after that business with the keys, he might have accepted the "best friends" bit, if he hadn't caught the fierce, masculine, hands-off glare the photographer arrowed his way a few moments ago. Whatever relationship Allie might think she had with the man, he wanted a hell of a lot more from her than friendship.

Surely she wasn't so naive that she couldn't see it? First with the Viking, and now with this character? She had to know simple friendship couldn't exist between the male and female of the species.

Maybe she didn't, Rafe conceded. Or maybe there wasn't room in her busy life for anything more. The dossier on her had included clippings that detailed a well-publicized engagement, and an equally well publicized breakup. Had her fiancé been one more in a string of "friends," or had he actually managed to penetrate Allie's formidable barriers and connect with the woman inside?

Rafe didn't think so. He'd known the woman for only one day, but his opinion of her had subtly altered in that short time. She collected men the way some people collected matchbooks. She couldn't help it. They did everything but sit up like eager, overgrown puppies and beg to be collected. Yet Rafe wasn't as sure as he had been last night that Allie made a game of them. After watching Eric the Blonde and Avendez in action, he was starting to believe they made games of themselves.

He'd have to be damn careful that he didn't do the same . . . which might be a hell of a lot easier said than done, he conceded. That one small contact with her smooth, satiny skin had generated an instantaneous and almost overwhelming urge to repeat the touch.

What he needed, Rafe decided, was a long walk in the cool night air, and a stiff drink, not necessarily in that order. Since he didn't allow himself to drink while on assignment, that left only one option.

He had to familiarize himself with the compound at night, anyway. He didn't anticipate having to make a middle-of-the-night escape with Allie, but he wanted the routes laid out in his mind, just in case. He didn't need another permanent and visible reminder of how dangerous it was to rely on only one escape route.

Besides, after the incident in the hangar this morning, he was beginning to realize how little he could anticipate, where Allison Fortune was concerned.

Four

Rafe would have been the first to admit that most of his knowledge of modeling had been gleaned from flipping through the swimsuit edition of *Sports Illustrated*. He soon learned that the impression he had of laughing women splashing thigh-deep in a sparkling sea while a photographer clicked away at two hundred miles an hour held little resemblance to the reality of the profession.

It was work. Damned hard work. And it required a level of discipline and endurance that astounded him.

The first day of the shoot began, as threatened, at five o'clock. Rafe rolled out of bed, instantly awake, but not particularly happy about it. Security considerations aside, this early-morning jaunt through the open countryside wasn't high on his list of fun things to do. He wasn't out of shape, exactly. He could sprint like hell when the occasion demanded, which it had in more than one memorable instance. But given a choice of exercise methods, he would have preferred a stationary bike... with Allie on the bike and him stationary.

After a quick trip to the bathroom, he pulled on the gray sweats he'd purchased from the resort's gift shop the evening before. Fortunately, the shop stocked an assortment of tennis shoes. Unfortunately, the only pair in Rafe's size were designer originals with purple-and-black zig-zags stitched across the yoke. He stood and stomped his feet. To his relief, the baggy sweats covered the tops of his insteps. He did a few quick knee bends to loosen up, then tucked his Smith & Wesson into the holster nestled at the small of his back. Moments later, he walked through the chill, splintering dawn to the next casita.

His faint hope that Allie might have reconsidered this jogging business faded as soon as she opened the door at his knock. She stood framed in the light spilling from the sitting room, and Rafe swallowed. Hard. She wore her hair pulled back in a loose ponytail, well-worn running shoes and a glistening pale green Spandex bodysuit that would have been a tight fit on a number three pencil.

"Morning," she said, stepping outside.

She turned to lock the door, giving Rafe an unimpeded view of her sloping back and her firm, rounded bottom. His hands curled into tight fists.

"Morning," he muttered.

She dropped the key into a flat pouch attached with Velcro to one hip. From the way the pouch bulged, Rafe assumed it also held the beeper. The thing certainly couldn't be concealed anywhere else on her person.

Propping a foot against the wall, she bent and pressed her cheek against her calf. In the process, she

stretched the Spandex and Rafe's lung capacity to their
limits. He must have made some inarticulate sound,
because she gave him a curious glance.

"Not a morning person?"

"Not any kind of a person without a couple of
ounces of caffeine slogging through my system," he
admitted, his voice gruff.

She switched legs, and Rafe's hamstrings twitched
in protest. "Well, there's a coffeemaker in my kitchenette, but we don't really have time now, if we're going to get in a run. Today's the first day of the shoot,
and we have to—"

"Stick to the schedule. I know."

She switched legs again, and Rafe felt his back teeth
grind. Her ponytail flopped as she twisted her face to
glance up at him.

"Don't you need to loosen up?"

He did. He most certainly did. But contorting himself over his thigh wouldn't accomplish the trick.

"I did some stretches in my room. I'll save the rest
of my energy for the real thing."

"You sure?"

"I'm sure."

She looked doubtful, but dropped her leg and
stepped away from the wall. "Okay. Do you want to
set the pace?"

"It's your exercise program. You set it. I'll let you
know if I can't keep up."

Rafe was still only halfway recovered from the
whammy of the glistening green Spandex when she hit

him with another. It soon became apparent that when the woman said she ran in the morning, she meant she *ran*. She started with an easy lope across the adobe-walled compound. Once outside the wooden gates, she sped up to a trot. A few moments later, she kicked into a fast jog. Then the narrow dirt road that led from the resort to the state highway a few miles away straightened out, and she hit her stride.

Within five minutes, rivulets of sweat were tracking down Rafe's neck. Within ten, he was sucking in razor blades instead of air. Gritting his teeth, he concentrated on putting one foot in front of the other and sweeping the terrain at regular intervals.

Overhead, the sky lightened from impossible shades of red and purple to a feathery, gold-streaked blue. A broad, flat blade of light cut like a sword through the pine-shrouded Sangre de Cristo peaks surrounding them. Suddenly, the high desert terrain at the base of the mountain took on a hundred different shades of dun and green. Silvery tumbleweeds piled one on top of the other where the wind had blown them, and stalks of tall, spiky, narrow-leafed yuccas thrust up like bayonets against the sky.

Nostrils flaring, Rafe dragged in the sharp, resiny scent of pines carried from the mountains by the morning downdrafts. He might have appreciated the grandeur of the world around him, if he had the energy or the breath to do so. Allie glanced over her shoulder a couple of times to see how he was faring. He had just decided to tell her he needed to slow it down when she moderated her pace and dropped back beside him.

"You okay?"

He didn't even consider going for macho. He wouldn't be much use to his client if his legs collapsed under him, which they might do if they didn't turn back soon.

"No."

He expected a smirk. At the very least a lift of a superior red-brown eyebrow. Instead, she gave him that half smile that he was coming to crave the way a chocolate junkie craves M&Ms.

"The altitude's getting to me, too. Want to head back?"

"Yes."

She swung around and retraced her steps. Following hard on her heels, Rafe couldn't help but note the smooth, rippling musculature of her back and bottom under their glistening green covering. He also noted that she hadn't worked up anything faintly resembling a sweat. Suspecting that the altitude hadn't gotten to her as much as his painful rasping, he set his jaw and calculated the distance to the resort's gates.

He could make it.

Maybe.

He might have . . . if his left leg hadn't chosen that moment to turn to iron. Excruciating pain wrapped around his thigh like a vise. Rafe's stride faltered, then went lopsided. He halted for a moment, and the gripping pain intensified. Grunting, he forced himself to resume his jerky movement.

At the sound of a grunt behind her, Allie spun around. She'd maintained too many unnatural positions for too many painful hours not to recognize instantly the signs of a world-class charley horse. She dashed back to Rafe, panting from the combination of thin air and exertion.

"Stop a minute. Let me massage the cramp."

Jaws tight, he shook his head. "It'll work itself out."

She danced around him. "Rafe, for heaven's sake! Stop!"

"It feels better," he got out through gritted teeth, "if I keep moving."

It might feel better at this instant, but Allie knew from bitter experience that a constant pull on protesting muscle could lead to a severe strain. Her mouth settled into a tight line, and a glint Rocky would have recognized instantly came into her eyes.

Her twin always claimed that she could tell the moment Allie decided to do something that would get them both into trouble. Usually, she'd try to talk Allie out of it, cite the dire consequences that might result. Then she'd grin and join right in. Rocky wasn't here to issue any warnings, however, and Allie planted herself squarely in front of Rafe.

At the least, she expected him to slow his pace. At the most, for him to bump into her. What she didn't expect was the unstoppable forward momentum of rock-solid body. He plowed into her before he could stop himself. Startled, Allie tried to disengage. She took an awkward hop back, his foot tangled with hers. Then they both went down.

Twisting in midair, he cushioned her fall with his body. Allie landed atop him with an "Oomph," and his arms locked around her with a force that squeezed the rest of her breath from her lungs.

"Don't ever try something...so stupid again," Rafe rasped out, his damp sweatshirt rising and falling like an accordion under her splayed fingers. "I could've hurt you."

Allie gasped and tried to drag some air into her starved lungs. "I . . . You . . ."

"What?"

She wiggled desperately and pushed at his chest with the heels of her hands. "I . . ."

"What, dammit?"

"I . . . can't . . . breathe!" she shouted, expelling the last of her oxygen in the process.

His arms loosened fractionally. Just enough for Allie to gulp down huge drafts of the New Mexico morning. Relief washed through her, and her rigid body went limp. Dropping her forehead to his shoulder, she lay sprawled atop him for long, life-giving seconds.

Gradually, her pulse slowed and her lungs stopped pumping like overworked bellows. When she felt reasonably certain she could speak with some coherence, she lifted her head.

"I'm sorry. I didn't mean to trip you."

One black brow shot up in patent disbelief.

"I didn't," she insisted, still panting.

She wiggled again, intending to slide off his chest. She was finding it entirely too difficult to pull together her scattered thoughts, much less form an adequate apology, with her hips grinding into his. To her surprise, he didn't release her. She glanced down at his face and saw his eyes narrowed to slits behind their ridiculously thick black lashes.

"Okay," she said, suddenly a little breathless again. "I'll admit it wasn't such a good idea to step in front of you in full stride. I just know how painful a muscle can be when it gets hard like that."

A wicked gleam leaped into the silvery blue eyes. "You do?"

Allie didn't have any difficulty interpreting the glint in his eyes. Nor would any other female. The man was as subtle as a locomotive lumbering down the tracks. She decided to meet the train head-on.

"Yes, I do. And don't try to twist my words into something out of *The Workingman's Guide to Sexual Doublespeak*. You know darn well I was talking about your cramp."

He shifted under her. Allie's fingers dug into the damp sweatshirt as he raised one leg, bracing her thigh against the hard wall of his.

"What cramp?"

She rolled her eyes. "I should know better than to try to communicate sensibly with a man in sweatpants and purple tennis shoes."

He gave her a slow, slashing grin that made Allie's heart stop, then skip a couple of beats.

"You noticed the shoes, did you?"

"They're a little difficult to miss," she retorted, fighting an answering smile. "They're a bit avantgarde for my tastes, but they'll go well with your tie."

His grin widened, and Allie couldn't help herself— she melted against him. That was the only word for it. The residual stiffness left her legs, and they tangled with his. Her breath eased out, sinking her stomach against his rib cage. And the arms she'd wedged against his chest sort of collapsed. Behind their shield of Spandex, her breasts flattened even more. Her nipples stiffened in protest, or maybe in response to the small groan that started low in his diaphragm and rumbled upward.

"Ah, Allie... This is probably one of the dumbest things I've ever done."

Allie wasn't sure whether he was referring to his purple shoes, their aborted run or the way he kept her pinned against him. Before she could decide, Rafe kissed her. One arm left her waist, a big hand curled around her neck, and then he brought her face down to his and kissed her.

Allie had been kissed before. A respectable number of times, as a matter of fact. But never while she was sprawled atop a sweaty male and lying in the middle of a dusty road. She didn't hear any violins or smell any roses in this scenario. Didn't see soft lights or savor the fizz of fine champagne. There was only a hard, suddenly urgent man who began by tasting her and was soon devouring her. Or she was devouring him. She didn't know who deepened the kiss, and she didn't care.

She cared when he ended the kiss, though. A lot. More than a lot. Shuddering, she drew in a ragged breath and opened her eyes.

"I was right," he told her, cradling her head with his hand.

Allie didn't pretend to misunderstand. The regret in his eyes allowed no misinterpretation.

"Dumb, huh?" she asked softly.

"Very."

"But . . . nice."

His fingers tightened on her scalp. "Very."

She nodded slowly, then eased one knee to the ground and pushed herself off his chest. When they were both standing, Allie forced herself to meet his gaze.

"Look, I won't take this out of context. We just got a little carried away by the—" she waved a hand to encompass the tumbleweeds and the dusty road "—by the dirt," she finished helplessly.

He lifted a hand and brushed a knuckle down her cheek, as he had last night. Allie willed herself not to curl her face into his hand.

"I got carried away by more than that. You're a beautiful woman, Allison."

He meant it as a compliment. Allie knew that. Intellectually she understood that the male of most species placed more value on coloration and plumage than the female did. She also understood that few women would sympathize with her irrational need for Rafe to see past the physical appearance she'd spent most of her adult life perfecting.

She understood all that, but disappointment still nibbled away at the remnants of her lingering pleasure. She summoned a smile.

"Thank you. Unfortunately, I have to make myself a lot more beautiful and don't have much time to do it. Is your leg okay?"

Rafe felt her withdrawal. It was subtle, like the curling of a rose to escape the cold. A part of him wanted to prevent her retreat. To bury his fingers in that loose, floppy ponytail, drag her against his chest and kiss her until her cheeks flushed with heat again and her eyes lost that cool distance.

The more rational part of his mind acknowledged that he'd almost lost one client, not to mention his own life, to a few seconds of careless inattention. He'd never forgive himself for missing the bomb that had engulfed their vehicle in flames. And he sure as hell wouldn't forgive himself if something like that happened to Allie.

God, he couldn't believe he'd wallowed in the dirt with her like that. A truck could have rolled right over them, and he wouldn't have noticed. Dusting himself off, he swore he wouldn't let Allie or his growing hunger for her distract him. Not while her father was paying him an obscene amount of money to protect her from some nut who wanted to do what Rafe had just done with her, and more. Much more.

"The leg's fine," he replied evenly. "Let's go."

"We'll take it easy. A slow jog."

She took the lead in her fluid, long-legged stride. After a half-dozen steps, Rafe decided he preferred their previous grueling pace. The agony in his lungs and throat generated by the hard run might have distracted him from the memory of Allie's slender body pressed against his... and from the ache in his groin area that sure as heck wasn't a charley horse.

Thankfully, they didn't have far to go. Moments later, they passed under the weathered timber arch of the gate. Once inside the adobe walls, they slowed to a walk. As Rafe forced his protesting legs to carry him across the courtyard, the lingering quiet of the early morning dissipated and the resort came awake.

A door in the main building slammed. A uniformed waiter called out a greeting as he trundled a cart laden with silver-domed dishes toward one of the outlying casitas. The fountain set squarely in the center of the yard gurgled and splashed water over its verdigris sides. Rafe and Allie were halfway across the courtyard when the door to one of the casitas opened and Xola stepped out. She carried a stack of hangers hooked over one shoulder and an assortment of shopping bags in her other hand.

"Hey, girl," she said to Allie, in that sexy, whiskey-dark voice that was so at odds with her short, nononsense brown hair and the faded T-shirt that enveloped her like a blanket. "Short run this morning?"

"Long enough," Allie replied, relieving her of some of her load.

The stylist grinned at Rafe, who took the rest of the crackling paper bags. "Poor baby, you look like hell warmed over. Did Allie run you into the ground?"

Rafe gave the universal response of every male to a question he either hadn't listened to or didn't want to answer. He grunted noncommittally.

"She will," Xola said with her throaty laugh. "Trust me on this. I've seen her in action. Did she tell you about the Olympic team?"

Rafe shot Allie an accusing look. "No, she didn't."

"We did an on-site shoot for a sponsor during the games," Xola explained. "Our model ran every day with one of the track stars. He swore she could've challenged Flo Joyner for her spot on the team."

"That was a few years ago," Allie commented. "I'm not quite in the shape I was then."

Xola's grin faded as she raked the length of Spandex with a frank, assessing glance. "So I see. You've put on a few extra pounds, haven't you? Better watch it, girl."

If Allie carried any excess weight, Rafe couldn't imagine where. A spurt of anger on her behalf shafted through him at the way her friends and associates felt free to criticize her. First Dom, with his crack about the lines in her face, and now Xola.

Unlike Rafe, Allie didn't appear to resent the criticism. "I've gained about five pounds," she told Xola evenly, "but then, I hadn't planned to do any more shoots."

"Well, Dom will sweat them off you in the next couple days. Ready to go to work?"

All business now, Allie nodded. "You can set up while I shower. Are the others stirring yet?"

As if on cue, a woman in a pale blue smock with the Fortune Cosmetics logo on the breast pocket walked around the corner of Allie's casita. She'd been introduced to Rafe briefly last night as Stephanie Something, the senior cosmetologist on Fortune Cosmetics's staff. An assistant lugging a heavy gray case emblazoned with the same logo trailed behind her.

"Mornin', Allie, Xola," Stephanie mumbled, clearly not yet awake.

She started to greet Rafe, but the words died as her gaze snagged at chin level, then hastily dropped. An awkward silence ensued, one Rafe had experienced countless times in the past three years. He would have ignored it, if he hadn't caught Allie's look and the fierce frown she gave Stephanie.

She was embarrassed for him, Rafe knew. He could shrug off the long, uncomfortable pauses, but others had trouble with them. His ex-wife had certainly never learned to handle the awkwardness. Her embarrassment had corroded into caustic bitterness and quickly destroyed what little was left of their marriage.

Defusing the situation with the ease of long practice, Rafe nodded to Allie. "You go on inside. I'll check the place, then grab some breakfast while you shower."

Her eyes troubled, Allie complied.

Fifteen minutes later, a waiter plunked down a platter the size of Rhode Island in front of Rafe, adding a warning that this season's batch of green chilis were hotter than the red. Rafe dug into the mound of eggs scrambled with diced peppers, *pesole,* and pork simmering in a spicy red sauce. He'd worked up an appetite during his short run.

For more than just spicy food, unfortunately.

His hand stilled with a warm rolled tortilla halfway to his mouth. That kiss had been a mistake. A bad one. He knew it before he'd even buried his hand in her silky hair. Now he'd had a taste of something sweeter than the honey dripping from his tortilla and a whole lot hotter than the green chili salsa slathered over his eggs. A taste of something he wouldn't sample again.

Aside from the fact that he owed it to his client to maintain a professional distance, that little scene with Stephanie Something in the courtyard had reinforced his determination to stay clear of entanglements. He didn't need Allie's pity, any more than he had wanted his ex-wife's.

Five

As Allie sluiced off the effects of her run and her tumble in the dust, the scene in the courtyard played and replayed in her mind.

She'd really handled that one well! So much for the vaunted sophistication that the media loved to play up in their endless stories about the princes and Wall Street potentates she supposedly kept dangling. Why in the world hadn't she gathered her wits quickly enough to fill the void left by Stephanie's inadvertent rudeness?

Probably because her wits were still wandering down a dirt road, trying to shake off the effects of Rafe's kiss.

He was right, Allie told herself as she squeezed shampoo onto her hair and worked up a lather. That kiss had been stupid. Extremely stupid. She'd known it even before she lowered her head and tasted the salty wonder of his mouth. Despite Rocky's prescription of a fast and furious affair, Allie didn't need a man in her life right now. Not when she had to concentrate all her energies on this shoot. And especially not with a man who had made it clear he didn't want any complications in his life, either.

Wishing she could rinse away Rafe's image as easily as the shampoo, Allie ducked her head under the spray. A few moments later, she wrapped one of the resort's huge towels around her underwear-clad body and padded on bare feet into her bedroom. Immediately the small group of professionals who'd been waiting for her sprang into action.

While Xola picked through the contents of her shopping bags for the accessories Allie would wear in this sequence, the cosmeticians spread their tools on a table by the window, where they could take advantage of the natural light. Allie sat unmoving while a hairstylist blow-dried her hair and piled it on top of her head. Shaking his head at the effect, the hairdresser let the heavy mass fall and went to work with a curling iron. Still unsatisfied with the result, he then attacked her hair with a boar-bristle brush and took out most of the curl.

When the temperamental hair designer finished, Stephanie and her assistant took over. Allie usually did her own makeup for modeling assignments, but this ad campaign was too important for her to trust her own hand. Brows furrowed in concentration, Stephanie applied a moisturizing base and a light matte foundation. She knew as well as Allie that a heavy foundation drew the camera's eye to the lines in the face. The real secret to beauty came in shading and highlighting. With an artist's skill, she wielded her brushes. When she finished, Allie surveyed the results in the mirror.

"It looks good, Steph. Very good."

"It better," the older woman said grimly. Like everyone else at Fortune Cosmetics, she knew how much depended on this new line of products.

While Stephanie packed her brushes and color kits into the case, Allie angled her head left and right to do another check. The smooth line of her jaw snagged her gaze, and she stilled. Unconsciously she lifted a hand to her throat.

Her features blurred in the mirror, and for a moment she saw not her face, but Rafe's. His clear steel-blue eyes. Tanned cheeks bristly with morning growth. His firm mouth. The puckered skin on one side of his chin and neck.

Allie's fingers pressed against the side of her throat. How ironic. Some people called her features perfect. She supposed a good number would consider Rafe's flawed. Yet she suspected they were far closer to equal inside than either of them had realized. They both wanted people to see past the outside shell to the person within.

Xola's face suddenly appeared in the mirror, startling Allie out of her silent contemplation.

"Are you ready for me?" the stylist asked impatiently. "If we don't want Dom squawking like a rooster with a severe case of gas all day, we'd better get you dressed and in position."

"I'm ready."

Tossing aside the towel she'd wrapped herself in, Allie stepped into the calf-length, taupe-colored suede skirt Xola handed her. Bending, she ducked her head so that the stylist could maneuver a white blouse with a lacy shawl collar over her hair. While Allie tucked the blouse into her waistband, Xola dug into her ubiquitous bags.

"Aha! Here it is."

Metal clanked against metal as she drew out a silver *concho* belt. Awed by the intricate workmanship on the shiny silver disks, Allie turned the belt over in her hands.

"This is gorgeous! Did you steal it, or break down and actually buy one of your props for a change?"

"I saw it in the gift shop late last night and sort of…borrowed it. Don't worry! I got permission from the janitor."

"Let's just hope he remembers to tell the gift-shop manager," Allie retorted.

Xola had gained a well-deserved reputation in New York for being able to procure any item for a shoot, from longhorn steers to miniaturized supercomputer conductors. Early in their association, Dom had stopped inquiring into her acquisition methods. As long as the police didn't show up at his studio to interrupt a shoot, he proclaimed, he didn't care where she acquired the props he wanted. Allie had her own thoughts about the acerbic insults stylist and photographer regularly traded. On Xola's side, at least, she suspected they constituted more than just professional give-and-take.

Xola wrapped the belt around Allie's waist and hooked the front clasp, then stepped back to admire her handiwork.

"Perfect! I had to remove three of the *conchos* to get it down to your size, but they slide right back on. Here, pull on your boots. We'd better haul our butts out of here before Dom has a coronary."

Rafe worked in a quick shower and a change after breakfast. Tucking his Smith & Wesson neatly into the holster strapped above his right ankle, he pulled on low-heeled boots, jeans and a white cotton shirt. He rolled up the sleeves for ease of movement and shrugged into his sleeveless sheepskin-lined vest as protection against the early-morning chill. A few moments later, he went outside to wait for Allie.

Propping a boot on one of the huge iron pots of geraniums placed under the arches in the walkway linking the casitas, he leaned his elbows across his knee and observed the flurry of activity at the far end of the courtyard. From this distance, he couldn't identify all the team members. The thin, worried-looking man Rafe thought was the advertising agency's art director. Or maybe the fashion editor. He hadn't fully sorted out the difference between the two positions.

Keeping everyone straight would require some effort. The technical side of the team included, among others, a couple of artists, Avendez and his swarm of assistants, and two computer-photo-imaging specialists from the Center for Creative Imaging in Camden,

Maine, who'd been flown in as special consultants. From the little Rafe had been able to glean about the center, it was unique in the world. Supposedly, it combined an array of new technologies in scanning, film recording, and high-resolution electronic cameras with state-of-the-art computer graphics.

Although Rafe had obtained a list of the entire crew before he left Minneapolis, he was still waiting for the results of the background checks he was having run on them. Any one of these characters could be Allie's caller, he thought. Any one of them could have fixated on her, or have some private reason to harass her. Any one of them could have wangled an excuse to be part of this team. He didn't exclude anyone, not even Avendez.

Particularly not Avendez.

When he heard the door of Allie's casita open, Rafe straightened. A small herd of professionals spilled out, carrying the tools of their trades. Xola flashed him a smile as she hurried by, and then his client stepped into the slowly warming sunshine.

Any man who wasn't completely blind would have gaped at her. Rafe possessed 20/20 vision.

This was the Allison Fortune the world usually saw. Glamorous. Confident. Her hair a smooth, shining cloak of dark red. Her brown eyes luminous.

Mentally he compared this perfect, shimmering beauty to the woman he'd seen dripping with lake water or streaked with road dust. It took him less than a second to decide which version of Allison Fortune he preferred. The one who'd rolled in the dust with him won hands down. It took him considerably longer to shove the image of Allie's whisker-reddened skin and flushed face, framed by a royal-blue sky, out of his mind.

"Still on schedule?" he asked, falling in step beside her as she crossed the compound.

"Barely, but I don't think we've been missed yet. It looks like Dom's still not quite set up."

From Rafe's perspective, it look like Avendez was several light-years away from being set up. The photographer stood in the middle of a crowd of technicians, waving his arms and shouting at them to get the damn strobes up and the generator going, now! In black pants and a white shirt and with his half head of flowing black hair, he reminded Rafe of a bad-tempered zebra.

Stepping over the cables that snaked like thick black spaghetti from the generator, Allie joined the group clustered by the wall. Rafe took up a position some yards away and watched Avendez bring order out of the chaos around him.

"All right, people. All right! Listen up, dammit! I want to get the first sequence done fast. We're going for a low-key shot with a natural effect, using the sky as the backdrop."

Rafe lifted a brow, amazed at the amount of equipment required to achieve this supposedly "natural" effect. In addition to the strobe lights mounted on portable scaffolding, a swarm of huge reflectors perched on stands like giant mosquitoes with their wings folded. Dom's senior assistant was bent over a huge trunk fitted with slotted trays that held an astonishing array of lenses and filters and God knew what else. They'd even shipped in a portable darkroom, Rafe noted, or at least he assumed that was the purpose of the small trailer nestled next to Avendez's casita. If there was anything left in the man's New York studio, it could only be the toilet.

Gathering his half head of black hair with a rubber band, presumably to keep it out of the camera's way, the Zebra jerked his chin at Allie.

"Let's get this show on the road. We'll start with the usual test shots. Let's have you leaning against the wall, chin up."

Allie walked to the waist-high wall that surrounded the sprawling hacienda. Leaning her hips against mud-colored adobe, she placed both hands behind her and lifted her face to the distant mountain peaks.

Xola adjusted the drape of her suede skirt, then stuck what looked like a bucketful of pins into the back of her blouse to take some of the fullness out of the collar. The hairdresser muttered something under his breath and attacked Allie with a brush in each hand. In seconds, her hair went from a smooth, shining curtain of dark red silk to something the man called unfettered. The makeup director in the blue smock swore when she saw the intensity of the lighting, and strode forward to swipe an assortment of brushes across Allie's forehead and chin.

All the while, Dom peered through the view finder of his camera and snarled at various assistants to dim the left strobe and raise the right reflector and to find his damned Zeiss macro lens! Finally he shouted at everyone to get the hell out of the way so he could get something on film before the sun changed their whole frame of reference, for God's sake.

"Bring your right hand up higher, Allie," he directed. "Higher. Tilt your head a little more to the left. Good. Now hold it."

Setting aside his camera, Dom snatched the Polaroid an assistant held at the ready. In rapid succession, he got off a half-dozen shots. Instructing Allie to hold her position, he then huddled with the art director to review the Polaroids.

From the conversations Rafe had overheard on the flight from Minneapolis, Fortune Cosmetics planned a massive blitz of every major women's magazine, with coordinated TV spots to follow. The print ad campaign would show the new beauty products in every sort of setting, from athletic to casual to business to formal. Santa Fe had been chosen as the site for the initial shoot because the city and its environs carried a cachet of sophistication, yet retained a sense of being close to the earth and sky. Something for everyone, Rafe thought, scanning the small crowd of guests and employees who'd gathered to watch the proceedings.

Rafe's review of the registration list with the manager yesterday afternoon had turned up one or two well-known names, which wasn't surprising for a resort that cost more per week than most people took home in a month. His contacts in Miami were running background checks on the entire guest list. He didn't think your average obsessed fan could afford to check into Rancho Tremayo for an extended stay, but he wasn't taking any chances.

An irate shout from the Zebra drew Rafe's attention back to the shoot. His face red, Avendez was gesticulating angrily at an assistant, a gangly young man in a burnt-orange University of Texas sweatshirt and a ball cap worn with the bill backward.

"Take that damn light meter, get your butt over next to Allie's, and give me an accurate reading this time!"

Apparently the test shots weren't "natural" or "low-key" enough for Avendez. Disgruntled, the photographer hunched over the viewfinder and fiddled with the huge lens protruding from his camera. Strobes were moved, dimmed, brightened. Filters were switched. The hairdresser darted in to unfetter Allie's hair some more.

Through the entire process, she didn't move. Her hands remained planted against the adobe wall, and her eyes stayed fixed on the jagged peaks of the Sangre de Cristos. After his recent bout with a cramped thigh muscle, Rafe could only admire her ability to command her body.

Finally, Avendez was ready for the real thing.

"Okay, Allie, do your moonling bit. Wipe your face clear. Clear, dammit! Come on, we don't have all morning!"

Eyes narrowed, Rafe watched Allie's expression. From where he stood, she didn't appear to move a single facial muscle. Didn't tighten or loosen her lips, or alter the angle of her eyes or chin. Yet her face seemed to take on an emptiness, like a pale white canvas waiting for the first stroke of a brush.

"That's better." The camera shutter clicked. "Now try for dreamy. Yeah, dreamy!" Click. "You got up at dawn, for God's sake. You're still half-asleep. Better. Hold it. Hold it." Click, click. "Now wake up a little. A *little!* Don't go bug-eyed on me. Just look like you have something better to do today than— Oh, hell! Xola, get that damned ruffle off her neck. Allie, hold the position."

While Xola adjusted the offending lace, Allie maintained her pose. Seconds, then minutes, dragged by. Rafe's muscles began to tense in sympathy. How the hell long was she supposed to keep her chin tilted up like that and her neck arched back?

For hours, it seemed, although it was probably only another ten or fifteen minutes. Then she and Dom began a choreographed, highly stylized dance that blended liquid movement, utter stillness and a range of expressions that ran the gamut from tender to playful to downright sensual.

"Bend to the left a little," Dom instructed. "Just a little. Good. Now show me some surprise. Surprise, not a gape! Good. Good. Hold it. Hooold it."

While Avendez shot eight or ten rolls with Allie in various poses against the wall, an assistant scurried to produce contact sheets after each roll. Between takes, the photographer and the art director examined the sheets with a magnifying glass, circled those shots they wanted printed, then shot more. It took three hours to capture the look Avendez wanted.

Then Allie moved from the wall to the tall gate and leaned against the weathered cedar beam, and the entire process began again.

With each passing hour, the sun heated the air until the early-morning chill was no more than a faint memory. In the process, the sky lost its dazzling clarity. Huge, puffy clouds built up as the warm air rose from the high desert plateau to clash with the cooler air at the tops of the peaks. Dom cursed with each shift in the light and took out his temper on the entire crew indiscriminately, until everyone but Allie glowered at him and at each other.

"I don't know how she does it," Xola muttered to Rafe after one trying episode. "Every day I work with the man, I swear it's my last. Allie just lets his temper roll off her back."

She let a lot of things roll off her back, Rafe noted. Endless criticism. Constant direction. The intent, intense professionals who swarmed around her like flies at every break in the shooting to repair her makeup or her hair or take light-meter readings.

"Tuck your chin, Allie," Dom snapped, oblivious of everything but the composition in the viewfinder. Rafe suspected a Tomahawk missile could plow into the dirt beside him and he wouldn't notice it.

"Bring it down a little more. More. Now look to your right. Jesus, your other right!"

In a languid movement, Allie tilted her head in Rafe's direction. Her eyes flickered for an instant as they snared his.

"Let's have a smile. No, not that one! That's the one you'd give your maiden aunt from Hoboken. Give me sultry. Give me the one every man wants to take to bed with him. That's better. Hold it. Hold it."

Rafe stiffened as Allie slanted him the kind of smile a man dreams of getting from a woman he's touched and kissed and rolled around in the dirt with. The kind that said she was ready to do it again, any time he wanted. He wanted. Lord, he wanted.

"Now more. More. Come on, Allie. Give. Oh, yes, that's good! Hold it. Hold it."

Perspiration slicked Rafe's palms.

"A little more to the right. Hold it."

His loins tightened.

"Drop your chin another notch. Hold it. Hold.... Oh, hell, I'm out of film."

For an instant longer, Allie's eyes held Rafe pinned, like a rare species of insect mounted on a board. Neither of them moved. Rafe didn't breathe. He couldn't.

Then she blinked and slowly straightened.

Only then did Rafe realize that the locked thigh muscle he'd experienced this morning was mild compared to what he was experiencing now. With a concentrated effort, he relaxed his wire-taut body. The idea that this woman could exercise such power over him with just a look and a smile shook the hell out of him.

Her back to Rafe, Allie clutched her hands together to hide their trembling. Good grief, did the man have any idea of how much he could affect her with just a look? She hoped not. She sincerely hoped not. She hadn't felt this shaky since she'd started school without her twin glued to her side. Rocky had come down with the flu, the rat, and left Allie to face the terrors of first grade alone.

What *was* this fascination she seemed to have with Rafe Stone? Usually she was able to blank her mind during a shoot and make lists of the things she had to do, like pick up the laundry or sweep the dust balls from under the sofa before her mother's next visit to New York. Today, her mind refused to blank.

Allie was used to people watching her during a shoot. *Everyone* watched her during a shoot, for heaven's sake. Usually with eyes trained to detect the slightest ripple of a shadow on her skin or a setting that overpowered the subject. During a studio shoot, the professionals picked her apart and put her back together again. On location, small crowds gathered, as they had here. Allie had never been distracted by either sharp-eyed technicians or gawking spectators before.

But Rafe Stone distracted her. Big-time. When she caught his steady gaze a few moments ago, she'd felt the jolt clear through the invisible shield she always erected between herself and the faces ringed around her.

For a few moments, she'd followed Dom's instructions instinctively. As ordered, she'd smiled. She'd thought about the way Rafe had kissed her this morning, and smiled. Only somehow the kiss had taken over where the smile was supposed to leave off.

Focusing on that kiss was really...dumb, she told herself. About as dumb as letting it happen in the first place. The next time Dom wanted sultry, she'd think about...About...Something!

Dom snarled an inarticulate order at his assistant and snatched his camera out of his hands. Stomping back to the gate, he glowered at his model.

"You ready?"

Allie drew in a steadying breath and turned her head so that Rafe wasn't anywhere within her peripheral vision.

"I'm ready."

The shoot would keep her busy, she told herself. The shoot, and her nightly sessions with Dom and the others, going over the contact sheets and the next day's schedule. Except for the early-morning run, she wouldn't be alone with Rafe. And she'd make damn sure he warmed up before they started, so that his leg didn't draw up in another cramp.

After the shoot, maybe she'd have time to sort out this illogical, persistent attraction she felt for the man. After the shoot, she might call him, or look him up when she was in...

With a start, Allie realized she didn't know anything about Rafe Stone. Where he was from. Where he'd gone to college. Whether he'd gone to college. How he'd become so scarred. She swallowed suddenly. She didn't even know whether or not he was married.

"Allie, for God's sake!" Dom shouted. "We're trying to convince people to buy this makeup for their faces, not use it to clean toilets. Get rid of the sour look and give me some charm."

Behind a face carefully reconstructed for charm, Allie's mind worked furiously. How could she have been crazy enough to squirm all over a man she knew nothing about? How could she be so... all right, so attracted to him? She'd been burned once by a fiancé she thought she knew and discovered she didn't know at all. Maybe she ought to make a phone call and get someone to do a background check or two, as Rafe had done on the resort's guests. As he'd done on her and her family, he'd casually informed her.

But who could she call? Not Rocky. Her twin would never let Allie live down this sudden curiosity about the so-called goon's personal life. Certainly not Jake. Her father would want to know why, and Allie hadn't been able to share her personal thoughts with him since he'd started substituting his work for his family.

Her brother Adam, maybe, or her older sister, although Caroline had worries enough without Allie piling a personal quest on top of them. But her cousin Michael, now...

"Charm's not your strong suit today, Allie," Dom said in disgust. "Let's try for happy. Good. That's good. Tilt your head to the left. Left, dammit! Now hold it. Hooold it!"

Workaholic, entrepreneurial Michael, Allie thought gleefully. Fortune Cosmetics's vice president for product development. He could find out anything and everything about Rafe Stone. Or his oh-so-efficient secretary could. Julia Chandler knew her way around the business world as well as her boss did. Allie would give her or Michael a call when they broke for lunch today. Assuming they ever broke.

She snuck a peek at Dom and bit back a sigh at his scowling face.

Not for a while yet, apparently.

Six

During the next few days, Rafe kept Allie within visual range fourteen to sixteen hours a day, but they were alone together only during the quiet moments just after dawn. The arrangement suited Rafe just fine. Given the fact that he couldn't wipe the feel or the taste of her from his mind, he didn't need time alone with her. Still, he found himself forcing his protesting lungs and legs to extend their run a little more each day.

He pushed himself for Allie's sake, or so he told himself. The woman was surrounded from dawn to the time she firmly shut her casita door at night, insisting on eight hours of sleep before the next day's shoot. The only time she really let herself go, the only time she could be herself, was during this hard, driving run. For these few moments, she didn't smile or tuck her chin or tilt her head, as directed. She didn't slip on dark glasses to keep her makeup from melting between takes. She put her face to the sun and ran.

By the fourth morning, Rafe still wheezed like an old-fashioned steam engine, but he managed to keep up. Puffing slightly, he ran beside her and feasted on the face turned up to the sun. With makeup, it was flawless. Without, it was damn close. Yet he'd discovered during the past few days that Allie viewed her stunning beauty with a down-to-earth practicality. She accepted it as a gift, like a musician's ear or a singer's voice, and disciplined herself as rigorously as any talented artist would to keep his skills finely tuned.

Her patience and grace under fire amazed Rafe. She never bristled defensively at the criticism that came from everyone from Avendez to the rancho's handyman, who'd dropped by one afternoon to watch a shoot. Rafe, on the other hand, was having to clench his jaw more and more often these days to keep from telling them all to back off. Remembering a particularly vituperative session, he grunted.

Allie threw him a quick glance. "You okay?"

"No."

A small smile tugged at her mouth. "Want to head back?"

"Yes. But let's see if we can make it to the state road first."

"Keep this up, Stone, and you might just start to enjoy running."

"Don't bet on it."

Her laughter floated up to him. With a start, Rafe realized this was the first time he'd heard her laugh. His jaw squaring, he put one foot in front of the other. Clouds of dust puffed with each step. Cool morning air lanced into his lungs with each breath.

He'd make the state road if it killed him.

It didn't, but he was sure glad when they reached their goal and turned around to head back. Once through Rancho Tremayo's gates, they slowed to a walk to cool down. Side by side, they crossed the courtyard.

Rafe sniffed appreciatively at the tantalizing aroma of frying onions that drifted from the main kitchen. A loud, long rumble from the vicinity of his stomach signaled its demand for immediate replenishment of the calories he'd just burned off.

"Sure you don't want me to bring you some breakfast?" he asked Allie. "A *real* breakfast."

Her nose wrinkled. "You're not really going to chow down on fried onions before seven o'clock in the morning, are you?"

"What are *huevos rancheros* without onions?"

"I wouldn't know."

He halted in mid-stride and swung her around. "Are you telling me you've never tasted fried eggs served on tortillas? With frijoles and chili sauce piled on them? Topped by onions and cheese and everything else left over from the night before?"

She shuddered. "Rafe! I'm from Minnesota. When I'm not on the road, I live in Manhattan. Where would I find fried-egg tortillas? Assuming I wanted to, of course, which I don't."

"Well, you can find them here. Come on, you've got to experience at least a taste of New Mexico."

She resisted, as Rafe had expected her to. "I can't. Not this morning, anyway. The crew will be waiting.

Maybe...maybe tomorrow? If we get up a little earlier and get our run in first?"

Rafe groaned. "You drive a hard bargain, woman."

"Well?"

"Okay, okay," he groused, falling into step beside her. "It's a date. But I'd better warn you the chef has promised to stir up a mess of *chilaquiles* for me."

"What are those?" she asked warily.

"You'll find out."

"Give me a clue. Animal, vegetable or mineral?"

"All of the above."

She swiped a stray strand of sweat-dampened hair out of her eyes. "I'm starting to have second thoughts about this."

"Too late. A promise is a promise."

Rafe left her at the door to her casita still trying to worm the ingredients out of him, and went to scarf down a small mountain of fried eggs and tortillas. Then he showered and joined the rest of the crew for the trip into Santa Fe for the day's shoot.

Allie couldn't concentrate.

It wasn't the traffic moving around Santa Fe's glorious old plaza that bothered her. The milling tourists of every nationality who had gathered to watch the shoot didn't distract her. Nor did Dom's scowls and the technicians' repeated adjustments to her face and hair and adornments disturb her.

The problem was Rafe.

Although she tried to blank him out of her mind and keep him out of her line of sight, she found herself watching for a glimpse of his blue-black hair out of the corner of her eye. He stood a little apart from the busy crew, his eyes shielded from the dazzling sunlight by aviator-style sunglasses as he surveyed the scene. He caught more than a few stares himself, Allie noted, her mouth tightening as a tourist frowned at his profile, then hastily averted his eyes when Rafe glanced his way.

"Loosen up, Allie," Dom snapped. "We're trying to sell lipstick, not Pepto-Bismol."

Relaxing her mouth, Allie gave her attention to the photographer. Their routine was too familiar to engage her full mind for long, however. While a part of it recorded Dom's instructions and responded with the requisite moves and expressions, a rebellious corner kept returning to Rafe.

In jeans and boots and a white shirt that strained across his shoulders, he looked rugged and at home in these surroundings. His dark hair and tanned skin carried a hint of the proud peoples who had once roamed this land at will, before the arrival of the Spanish conquistadores. Or he might have been one of the cowhands who'd driven their herds up the Santa Fe Trail. Allie could imagine him joining the tough, fiercely independent men who'd celebrated reaching the end of the trail in the gambling halls she'd been told had once lined the plaza. Yes, she could see Rafe drinking and playing monte and dancing with sloe-eyed señoritas in black veils who...

"Allie, for God's sake!" Dom snarled. "The light patterns are shifting enough without you adding to the problem. Hold still. Oh, hell, there's dust on the filter. I need to change it. Hold it a minute."

The minute stretched into two, then to three, as Dom swore at his assistant for handing him an ultraviolet filter when he wanted clear, dammit, clear! The muscles in Allie's back began to ache. She eased her position slightly and set off another tirade when Dom squinted into the viewfinder and found that his reference points had shifted.

By the time they finally wrapped it up for the afternoon, even Allie's patience was strained. Dom had become unbearable these past few days. He didn't speak ten words to Rafe during the shoots or the evening postmortems, but neither did he bother to hide his resentment of her bodyguard's constant presence. Rafe, on the other hand, ignored him, which only irritated the photographer more.

Dom's mood took a turn for the worse, if that was possible, when Xola reminded him about the party the resort manager had insisted on throwing for them that night. Not the most sociable of animals to begin with, Dom didn't want to shut down the shoot to go to a bleeping party.

By unspoken, unanimous vote, the crew gave Allie the unenviable task of convincing the photographer that everyone needed a break. He eventually conceded, but not graciously. In fact, Allie told him in exasperation, he made the fuzzy, saucer-size tarantula that had crawled into his camera case this morning seem positively congenial by comparison.

As a consequence, by the time their small convoy drove through Rancho Tremayo's gates, the entire crew was strung tight.

Rafe included.

The easy camaraderie he'd experienced with Allie earlier in the morning had completely dissipated during the exhausting day. He'd contacted the Santa Fe police to advise them of her situation soon after their arrival. They'd been cooperative about keeping in touch with NYPD on the status of the investigation and adding an officer for crowd control during the downtown shoot. Even with the extra set of eyes, though, Rafe was coiled tight from a day of scanning the crowds of tourists who gathered to watch the shoot.

His mood hadn't improved as the day stretched beyond the projected time and Avendez pushed for one more shot, one more pose. Like a sleek Thoroughbred bred for endurance as well as speed, Allie put herself through her paces. She was as tireless as the Zebra, or so it appeared.

But when Rafe arrived to escort her to the party that night, he noted an uncharacteristic droop to her shoulders. Drawing her elegant carriage around her like a cloak, she summoned her company smile and invited him in.

"You don't have to do that," he said as he stepped through the door. "Not with me."

"Do what?" she asked, startled.

"Put on your public face."

She studied him for a moment, as if trying to gauge the reason for his brusque comment. Then she shrugged. "This is the only face I have."

"You've got one for every occasion. And for every mood."

An emotion Rafe couldn't quite interpret darkened her eyes briefly. "You're wrong, but I'm not going to argue with you. I've had enough arguing for one day. Let me get my purse and we'll go."

She crossed the sitting room to pick up a small black leather bag, and Rafe realized that his night was going to be even longer than his day.

A week ago, even a few days ago, he would have reacted to this sophisticated creature with an instinctive, gut-level male response. His body would have tightened at the vision of her face framed by a tumble of dark red curls. His pulse would have hit Mach 3 at the expanse of creamy skin left bare by the sloping cowl neckline of her sparkly emerald-green sweater. He didn't even want to think about his lower organ's response to a strip of black leather so short it could hardly be called a skirt, or to those long, long legs encased in black tights.

Tonight, that small sag to her shoulders bothered him more than her stunning appearance. Or so he thought . . . until Allie bent over to pick up her purse.

Grimly he escorted her to the resort's main building. Who the hell did he think he was kidding? His body was so coiled he could barely put one foot in front of the other. His pulse jackhammered in his chest, and sweat had popped out on his brow the moment he glimpsed that damned skirt. He was a man, and Allie was all woman. She was more than that. She was Allie.

It didn't help Rafe's mood that every other male at the party saw the woman in her, as well.

The resort manager glommed on to her the moment she stepped into the long hall with the low stuccoed ceilings supported by weathered beams. Tall, tanned and manicured to perfection, the man reminded Rafe of a hair-sprayed Cuban cigar. An El Tampico, he decided objectively. With a thin, fine outer wrapper—and a dull inner taste.

"Miss Fortune! We've been waiting for you. Come and meet some of the other guests."

Rafe propped his shoulders against the wall and watched El Tampico parade Allie around the hall like a prize heifer at a cattle auction. Rafe had made some discreet inquiries about the man soon after their arrival. The nephew of a hotel magnate, he'd come out to prove himself by managing this exclusive resort some five months ago...leaving his wife and children in Dallas. He certainly wasn't thinking about the little woman now, Rafe noted sourly. Nor were any of the men circling Allie like vultures who'd just spotted their next meal.

This was how he'd first seen her, Rafe remembered. Surrounded by men at the Fortunes's party. The Viking had hung on her elbow then, the way the Cigar did now. Annoyance curled deep inside Rafe, then spiked to irritation when the Zebra strolled over to Allie and looped an arm around her neck. From this distance, Rafe couldn't tell what he said to her, but she laughed and kissed him on the unfurred side of his head.

"Can I buy you a margarita?"

The low, liquid voice at his side could have been poured from a bottle of honey. Rafe turned and glanced down at the woman next to him, who stood almost as high as his armpit.

"A Coke, maybe," he replied with a smile. "Better yet, a cup of coffee."

Xola's brows brushed the edges of her short-cropped brown hair. "Can't drink on duty? Poor baby. I don't think I could face tomorrow without a couple of margaritas. Dom outdid himself today."

"So why do you stay with him? From what I've gathered, you're good at what you do. Very good."

Xola's velvet chuckle poured out, jerking more than one man's head around. Rafe caught the looks of amazement as the resort's guests connected that liquid, sensual laughter with the woman who stood at his side, her stocky figure draped in a fringed Spanish shawl twice her size.

"Sweetheart, I'm the best stylist in the city, which means I'm the best in the universe. Any prop I can't find doesn't exist. Unfortunately, Dom's also the best, which is why I work with him. At least—'' her gaze slid to the far end of the room ''—he is when he works with Allie.''

Rafe studied her face for a moment, then asked quietly, ''Does Avendez know you're in love with him?''

Her gaze flew back to his. ''Are you kidding? I could wear a neon sign advertising the fact, but Dom wouldn't notice. He doesn't know any woman exists but Allie. I wish I could hate her.''

''Don't you?''

''No, I don't. Allie's one of the few models I know who doesn't actually believe the attention lavished on her has anything to do with her as a person. Besides,'' Xola added, with one of her patented stomach-tickling chuckles, ''if it weren't for Allie's calming influence on Dom, I probably would have thrown the switch on all his strobe lights and sizzled him to a half-bald bacon strip by now.''

Rafe grinned down at her. ''Sounds like a great idea to me.''

As she watched from across the room, Allie's fingers tightened on the stem of the margarita glass the resort manager had thrust into her hand. Rafe's slashing grin sent a stab of irritation through her. That was the same grin he'd turned on her, she thought in annoyance, just before he kissed her. Frowning, she rolled her shoulders to ease the weight of Dom's arm.

He shot her a sour look and strolled off. Allie barely registered his departure.

Xola and her bodyguard always seemed to find something amusing to chat about. Allie hadn't missed the stylist's habit of gravitating to Rafe's side during shoots. Any more than she could miss his obvious enjoyment of her company now. He certainly couldn't accuse Xola of wearing more than one face, she thought with a touch of spite. She looked exactly the same, morning and night.

Shame swept through her at the thought. Jealousy, Allie discovered, wasn't a very pleasant emotion. Particularly when she didn't have any right to be jealous. Rafe had been hired to spend his waking hours with her, and he performed his job with quiet efficiency. That didn't mean he had to stay glued to her side. He had every right to enjoy another woman's company.

"I have to confess something, Miss Fortune," the unctuous resort manager murmured in her ear. "I wangled a few of the shots of you taken around the resort."

Allie nodded absently, her eyes on the unlikely couple at the other end of the room. Rafe practically had to bend double to hear Xola over the background music.

"Would you mind autographing a picture for our rogue's gallery? I'll put you up right next to the vice president. He and his family stayed here a couple of months ago."

"What?" Allie dragged her attention back to the man at her side. "Oh, of course."

"I've got them in my office. Here, let me take that for you."

He eased the margarita glass from her hand and set it on the table beside her small bag. Distracted and irritated anew by the sight of Rafe's white teeth gleaming in another one of those incredible no-holds-barred grins, Allie let the man take her elbow and steer her through the crowd. The noise of the party faded as they walked into his large, paneled office.

"The photographs are on my desk. Here, which one do you like best?"

Allie shuffled through the prints, all of which had come from Dom's reject pile. She tapped a nail against a glossy shot of her face and shoulders silhouetted in Rancho Tremayo's timber-framed adobe gate.

"This one, I think."

The manager's arm brushed hers as he bent to examine her choice. "Yes, that's great. Here's a pen."

Allie took the heavy silver pen he offered and edged a bit to the side to give herself writing room. She leaned over to scrawl Best Wishes across a corner of the picture, then froze when his arm brushed her hip. Only this time, the contact was deliberate. It couldn't be anything else, since his hand stayed planted at the back of her leather skirt.

"If you don't get your hand off me," she said pleasantly as she scrawled her name across the print, "I'll break your arm."

He jerked away, stammering. "Uh...I was... just..."

She straightened. "I know what you were *just.*"

"I'm sorry, Miss Fortune. Really. You misinterpreted my eagerness over the photo."

"I obviously misinterpreted something." She tossed the pen onto the desk and gave him a look that combined disdain, haughtiness and plain old-fashioned dislike. "Let's get back to the party."

She swung around, prepared to sweep out of the room. The sight of Rafe leaning negligently against the doorjamb brought her to an abrupt halt.

He didn't say a word to the manager. He didn't have to. One look at Rafe's face had the man stuttering again. "We, uh... Miss Fortune was just..."

"Yes?"

Allie had always considered the term "dark and dangerous" a romantic cliché. At that moment, she understood that every cliché was originally based on a hard, cold fact. Rafe's leashed anger was all the more frightening for its rigid control.

The manager's Adam's apple bobbed several times. "Miss Fortune autographed a publicity shot for me. We, ah, were about to return to the party."

"You return to the party. I'd like to talk to my client a moment."

Visibly relieved, the man abandoned the scene without so much as a backward glance. Allie stiffened as Rafe's blue eyes raked her with an icy anger.

"I thought we had an understanding," he said coldly. "No more strolls in the dark without your chaperon?"

"My chaperon was otherwise occupied," she returned sweetly. Too sweetly.

His eyes slitted. "Not too occupied to see you slip out of the party with your friend. And without this."

He held up his hand, dangling her black purse.

Allie flushed. The sight of Rafe bending over Xola had disturbed her so much that she hadn't even thought about the purse. Still, that was no reason to feel so guilty about forgetting the beeper Rafe had insisted she carry. The office door stood wide open, for heaven's sake. A hundred or more people were congregated in the next room. One scream would have brought them running.

"All right. I forgot the rules. I forgot the beeper. I'm sorry."

"Sorry doesn't cut it in an emergency."

"Since this isn't an emergency, it will have to. I said I'm sorry. I'm not going to grovel."

He looked like he might try to make her do just that as he strode forward. Allie refused to retreat, although she thought about it for a second or two. Rafe could be rather intimidating when he chose.

"Dammit, Allie, you don't go anywhere without the beeper. *Anywhere!*"

"All right! I won't forget it again."

He tossed her the small bag. "See that you don't."

"Did anyone ever tell you that your client-employer communication skills need a little polishing, Stone?"

"Most of my employers," he returned, ushering her out of the office.

"Why doesn't that surprise me?"

Rafe knew damn well he was overreacting. He also knew that his fierce, blazing anger was directed at himself as much as at Allie. He still couldn't believe the searing male possessiveness that had streaked through him when he saw Allie stroll out of the party with El Tampico.

Leaving Xola in midsentence, he'd stalked across the room, snatched up Allie's purse and arrived on the scene just in time to hear her threatening to break the man's arm. She'd handled the Cigar easily, just as she had the Viking. That didn't mean Rafe liked seeing her do it. Any more than he liked the way men came on to her. Himself included, he remembered with a twist of disgust.

When he escorted his client to her casita an hour later, Rafe still hadn't shaken his residual anger. Neither had Allie, apparently. He made a quick, thorough check of the interior.

"Lock the door behind me," he instructed curtly.

Her response was even more curt, "I will."

"Keep the beeper within reach."

"I will."

"Good night."

"Good night."

Allie prided herself on the fact that she didn't slam the door behind him. She wanted to, though. She certainly wanted to.

Thoroughly disgruntled, she walked into the bedroom and kicked off her shoes. She started to toss the black bag on the chair, but halted in midswing. Making a face, she dug the beeper out and set it on the nightstand, between the phone and the little tin carousel. What a rotten end to a day that had begun with a slashing grin from Rafe and a promise of *chila*-somethings.

After changing into her sleepshirt and scrubbing her face and teeth, she padded, barefoot, back into the bedroom. Her hand hovered over the phone for a few moments, then dropped. She and Rocky usually talked to each other every day. In true twin fashion, they didn't really need to communicate so much as to simply link up with their other half.

Tonight, though, Allie couldn't quite bring herself to call her sister. Rocky would hear Allie's simmering anger instantly. Worse, she'd pick up on her sister's lingering jealousy and confusion. Like a lioness pouncing on her prey, she'd gleefully tear every detail of the evening out of her twin. She hadn't had the least difficulty dragging out the details of that kiss.

Allie wasn't ready to talk about tonight, not even to Rocky. Especially not to Rocky. She needed time to sort out her confusion. She needed to understand just how Rafe Stone could irritate and distract and anger and fascinate her, all at the same time. How she could feel jealous of the smile he gave another woman, and ache for the kiss they'd both decided had been a mistake.

Sighing, Allie wound the toy carousel. A Chopin polonaise filled the air as she switched off the light and slid under the covers.

The buzz of the phone jerked her awake some time later. Groggy with sleep, she groped on the nightstand beside her bed. Her flailing hand knocked into the carousel. It tinkled once or twice, the small sounds almost lost as the phone buzzed again.

With a muttered oath, Allie sat up and fumbled for the lamp switch. Shoving her hair out of her eyes with one hand, she snatched up the phone with the other.

"Hello," she mumbled, still half-asleep.

A long, heavy silence drifted through the earpiece. Allie frowned, trying to gather her sleep-heavy senses.

"Rocky? Is that you?"

"No, Allison."

The slow, heavy whisper sent a wave of icy cold through Allie.

"Did you make love to the camera today, Allison? The way you always do? The way I want to make love to you?"

Allie's first instinct was to slam the receiver down. At the last second, she curtailed it. Gripping the phone in a white-knuckled hand, she grabbed the beeper and squeezed it as hard as she could.

Seven

Allie was still sitting in the middle of the bed, the phone clutched in one hand and the beeper in the other, when Rafe came in low, a gun gripped in both hands. If the obscenities Allie had forced herself to listen to hadn't already shaken her badly, her bodyguard's dramatic entrance would have done the trick.

In jeans and an unbuttoned shirt he'd obviously dragged on while on the run, he was all lean, coiled power, bare chest and cold blue steel. Allie shrank back as the gun in his hand swung in a short, deadly arc. He searched the shadows, then pinned her to the sheets with a narrowed stare.

"What's going on?" he asked tautly.

Her hand shaking, Allie held up the instrument. The beep-beep-beep and recorded message advising that the receiver was off the hook sounded tinny in the taut stillness of the room.

"It was..." She wiped her tongue around her lips. "It was him. I listened... I tried to keep him on, but... he hung up."

Rafe lowered his weapon and reached for the phone. She couldn't seem to let go.

"Come on, Allie," he said gently. "Let me have it."

"I..." She stared helplessly at the instrument in her hand. "I, uh,..."

Swearing, he set the gun on the nightstand. "It's okay," he murmured, unlocking her fingers. "It's okay. I'm here. He can't hurt you."

Shudders racked her, one after another. "He doesn't want to hurt me. That's what he said. Not... not unless he has to."

With another curse, Rafe pried the beeper out of her white-knuckled fist and tossed it onto the nightstand. Then he folded her into his arms.

Trembling uncontrollably, Allie pressed herself against the hard wall of his bare chest. She wouldn't cry. She wouldn't give the pervert that satisfaction. But she couldn't seem to stop shaking. She wrapped her arms around Rafe, wanting, needing, an anchor.

He understood her need. Dragging her into his lap, he held her tight with an arm around her waist. His other hand cradled the back of her head. Her nose found the junction of his neck and shoulder, left accessible by the open shirt. With a sound that was half whimpering fear, half relief, she buried her face in his smooth, warm skin.

He rocked her, as a father would a small child. "It's okay, Allie. I'm here."

When he shifted a little, she clutched at him in panic.

"I'm not going anywhere," he assured her. "Not yet. I just want to call the hotel operator. Hang on, sweetheart."

Her hands twisting in his shirt, Allie clung to him as he reached for the phone.

"Miss Fortune just received a call at this number. Can you tell me if it came through the hotel's internal switchboard or from outside the resort?"

His voice was a low rumble against her ear. Allie closed her eyes and tried to concentrate on the erratic thump of his heart against his chest wall instead of the awful pounding of her own.

"Any way to tell if it was local or long-distance?"

She felt, rather than heard, his little grunt of disappointment.

"Yeah, well, thanks."

"They... they can't tell where it came from?"

"Only that it came from outside Rancho Tremayo."

"Great," she muttered against his collarbone.

His hand stroked her hair, strong and infinitely comforting. "You'll have to tell me what he said."

Shudders rippled through her. "Not yet. Please. I can't talk about it yet."

"When you're ready, sweetheart."

Allie wasn't sure she'd ever be ready. She didn't want to think about, much less repeat, the phrases that promised to make an obscene, frightening assault out of something that should be... should be beautiful. And warm. And slowly, sensually invasive. Like the rhythm of Rafe's heart against hers. The feel of his arms around her.

Gradually her shudders gave way to intermittent shivers. Slowly his scent replaced the coppery taste of fear as the focus of her senses. His shirt had been lightly starched. His skin carried a hint of rumpled covers and the cool night. Where her breath warmed it, the supple surface grew moist. Allie felt a sudden, unexpected urge to touch the tip of her tongue to the crease in his neck. She was as surprised as Rafe when she gave in to the urge.

The hand that had been stroking her hair went still. The muscles beneath her hands tensed. "Allie..."

"I know, I know," she murmured into his neck. "This isn't smart. This is world-class dumb. Don't worry, Rafe. I won't kiss you again."

She licked him instead.

Edging aside his shirt collar, she brushed her lips along the slope of his shoulder. Her tongue left a hot, wet trail across his collarbone. It amazed her that this simple exploratory act could lead to such explosive need. From a small taste came a desire to feast. Her mouth moved from his shoulder to his neck once more. Suddenly Allie understood the ageless lure of vampire fantasies.

His pulse throbbed just beneath the surface of his skin. Hot, heavy, fast. Could she claim him forever if she bit him, just a little? Just a nip?

This time it was Rafe who shuddered. When he would have pulled back, Allie curled her hands around his arms. Only then did she notice that his muscles had gone granite-hard. He was so taut. His skin so hot. A heady sense of power rushed through her. She'd never dreamed she could bring him, and herself, to such heat with just her lips and her tongue and her teeth.

Rafe couldn't believe it, either. He willed himself not to pull her head back and savage the mouth that shot fire into him with every touch, every tiny nip. He'd never realized that the hollow between his shoulder and neck was such an erogenous zone. Or that a woman could almost push him past all restraints with just the whisper of her breath against his skin.

His common sense told him to let her go. Now. Before he forgot she was his client. Forgot she'd just received a disgusting, possibly threatening call. One that needed to be documented before the details blurred in her mind.

The feel of her soft body against his completely drowned out the voice of reason. Cursing himself for his lack of restraint, Rafe tightened his hold. Without the barrier of Spandex to separate them, her heat flowed into his. Desire rose in him, heavy and urgent. He shifted her on his lap to ease the sudden constriction in his jeans.

Afterward, Allie was never quite sure how her nightshirt slipped down her shoulders. Or when Rafe's hand worked inside the soft cotton. At the time, her only interest was the scrape of his palm against the undercurve of her breast. Her nipple tightened in anticipation of his touch. She twisted in his hold, wanting that contact desperately. When his fingers teased the aching peak, she gasped in pleasure.

Wanting to give him pleasure in return, she slid her hand up his chest. Her fingers splayed through a light mat of springy hair. Smoothed across rounded pecs. Inched upward. Stilled when they encountered unexpected ridges.

Through the searing heat of his skin, Rafe felt her fingers hesitate on his scars. That small, brief pause brought him back to reality as nothing else could have. Fighting his body's driving need, he did what he should have done earlier. He eased her away from him.

She glanced up in surprise, her breasts quivering from the sudden loss of contact. Rafe's jaw locked so tight it ached when he saw the dark-tipped nipples he'd tugged and teased into stiff peaks. He dragged his gaze from the creamy breasts that fit so perfectly in his hand and met the confusion in her brown eyes.

"We can't do this, Allie. Not now."

The confusion in her eyes gave way to consternation.

"Listen to me, sweetheart. You're still shaking. You're upset. You need time to calm down, to think about this."

Allie bit down on the sharp retort that what she needed, desperately, was his body on hers. It didn't appear that she was going to get it. Her head whirling as much as her senses, she struggled to understand his withdrawal. He'd wanted her, as much as she wanted him, yet he'd pulled back. Again, damn him. Again.

Stiffening, she reached for the edges of her nightshirt to cover herself. When she tried to wiggle off his lap, he held her in place a moment longer.

"I wanted it, too," he admitted, assessing her reaction with an accuracy that had Allie squirming in embarrassment. "I still do. But we have to talk."

The only thing that saved her from total humiliation was the hoarse edge to his voice.

"I don't really feel like talking right now," she muttered.

If pressed, she couldn't have told him what she really felt like doing at this moment. It wavered somewhere between slinking away in abject embarrassment and slugging him.

"You've got to tell me what the caller said," Rafe insisted. "There might be something the police can use in his phrasing or his choice of words."

Knowing he was right didn't make it any easier to comply. Especially not with his hard thighs under her bottom. Allie wiggled again, seeking release. This time he let her go. Tugging her sleepshirt down to cover her hips, she moved a few steps away. With her gaze fixed on a mauve-and-blue print of a Pueblo woman, she recited as much of the call as she could remember, stumbling a bit over the more disgusting phrases.

Silence spun out for long moments after she finished. Then Rafe swore, viciously. Allie turned to find him stuffing his shirttail into his jeans.

"I'll sleep in the sitting room tonight. Will you be all right while I go back to my casita to get my gear?"

No, she wouldn't, but not for the reasons he thought. Allie suspected it would take her far longer to put the memory of his arms around her out of her mind tonight than it would the phone call.

"You don't have to sleep here. I'm all right."

"I want to be here if he calls again."

"He won't," Allie said flatly. "Not tonight, anyway."

"How do you know?"

"He never does. Besides," she added, her mouth curling in disgust, "he achieved the object of his call. He got off by frightening me. Only I'm not frightened anymore. I'm just mad."

And embarrassed. And confused. And more frustrated than she'd ever been in her life.

Twice now, she'd melted all over this man. Twice now, he'd withdrawn. The next time, she swore, he wouldn't pull away from her. The next time, Mr. In-Control Macho Man Stone wouldn't know what hit him.

Right now, though, she just wanted him out of her bedroom and out of her sight, before she made a fool of herself again by crying or swearing or otherwise letting him know he'd shaken her far more than her unwelcome caller ever could.

"It's late, Rafe," she said with a lift of her chin. "I need to get some sleep, or I'll have circles under my eyes tomorrow that even our new line of beauty products won't disguise."

"You sure you're okay?"

"I'm sure."

He hesitated, frowning, then gave a reluctant nod. "All right. Call me if you need me."

Oh, she needed him, Allie thought, She needed him in a way she didn't begin to understand. Unfortunately, he didn't seem to need her to quite the same degree.

She followed him into the sitting room and watched while he retrieved his key from the lock.

"You sure you want to run in the morning?" he asked, still frowning. "Maybe you should sleep in."

"I refuse to let this pervert throw me off stride or off schedule. Damn straight I want to run."

The frown eased into a wry grin. "I was afraid you'd say that. Just remember, after our run you're making your first acquaintance with *chilaquiles*."

"Right. The animal-vegetable-mineral dish."

Allie slid back into bed some moments later, completely drained. She'd run the gamut of emotions tonight, from anger at the resort manager and at Rafe to stark fear to stunning, soaring desire, bitter disappointment and embarrassment. Yet she found herself dwelling on a growing eagerness for a taste of something hot and spicy for breakfast.

She didn't get either her run or her first taste of the mysterious dish.

She and Rafe had just begun their warm-up exercises the next morning when the phone rang. Allie froze with her left cheek halfway down to her right calf. Before she could even unbend, Rafe had moved into the bedroom. Holding the extension in his hand, he signaled her to answer the phone in the sitting room.

Allie swallowed and picked up the receiver at the same instant Rafe did his. Before she had it halfway to her ear, Dom's voice leaped out at her.

"Have you seen this sunrise? It's unbelievable. I want you outside in twenty minutes."

"Dom, I'm not dressed!"

"I don't need you dressed. Wear a goddamn sheet if you want. No, put on something black. I don't care what. I just want your eyes. Move it, Allie."

She winced as he slammed the receiver down. Replacing hers with a bit more care, she gave Rafe a small, lopsided smile.

"You'd better go grab a cup of coffee and some of those *chila*-whatevers while you can. If I'm not mistaken, all hell's going to break loose around here in about ten minutes."

Sure enough, Xola and Stephanie and the rest of the prep crew descended on the casita within moments. Like Allie, they were in varying states of undress. Unlike Allie, they weren't happy about turning out to enjoy a spectacular New Mexico dawn. In a flurry of brushes and moisturizer pads and scathing remarks about photographers who demanded the impossible, they went to work.

Twenty minutes later, Rafe propped a shoulder against an archway, sipped from a steaming cup of coffee and watched Avendez position Allie. Wrapped in a black cloak Xola had miraculously procured from some unspecified source, she stood with her face to the dark mountain peaks in the west. Behind her, blazing color pinwheeled across the eastern sky. It was the kind of sunrise only New Mexico could produce.

The swirling, brilliant hues had to do with the altitude, Rafe had learned. The lowest point in New Mexico was over a thousand feet higher than the loftiest peak in the Ozarks. At this height, the air was so thin, so lacking in oxygen and carbon dioxide, that it offered little to diffuse or defract the light. Instead of glowing softly, streetlights became pinpoints of brilliance in the night. White buildings set against the dark green backdrop of ponderosa pines could be seen for thirty or more miles away. Sunrises and sunsets became awesome displays of reds and purples and golds, with slashes of turquoise thrown in.

Reluctantly Rafe conceded that the agony this thin air caused him during his early-morning runs with Allie might be a small price to pay for something that could only be classified as one of the wonders of the natural world. The question yet to be answered in his mind, however, was why Avendez had been up so early to view this particular display.

If he was up at five, had he also been up at two, when Allie's call came in?

It was a definite possibility. The man drove himself as hard as he drove everyone else. He locked himself away in his portable processing center for hours after each day's shoot, harassing his assistants while they developed contact sheets and consulting with the art directors. He often went back to the center after his nightly review sessions with Allie to work.

Rafe had checked out the processing unit during the first day's shoot. The place was self-contained and Saturday-morning-inspection neat. Chemicals were stored in clearly marked containers and film supplies and equipment were locked away. A dark room took up the back half of the unit. The front half served as an office and design center, complete with several computers and, Rafe remembered suddenly, a phone.

Stiffening, he eyed the swarm of people clustered around Allie. Then he tucked his hands in the pockets of his sheepskin-lined vest and strolled toward the processing center. With the shoot just reaching its full frenzy, no one noticed him slipping inside.

The portable phone nested in its own black leather case. Powered by a rechargeable battery pack, it emitted a low hum when Rafe lifted the receiver. For a mobile phone to operate, it had to be keyed to a local service. Or to a nationwide service that charged a "roaming" fee for use outside the home area. If someone had made a call from this phone to Allie's room at approximately two-twenty this morning, there'd be a record of it.

His jaw tightening, Rafe wrote the number on a slip of paper. A phone tap required a court order. A check of telephone call records required only a few friends or a contact in the police department.

Tucking the phone number into his vest pocket, Rafe made a quick survey of the processing center. Nothing had changed from his first visit to the unit, except...

He opened the left panel of a wall-mounted display board and felt the breath leave his lungs. Photographs of Allie filled the surface. Hundreds of photographs, large and cropped, color and black-and-white.

Allie laughing into the camera.

Allie staring dreamily into the distance.

Allie with her chin tucked and her lips curved and her eyes telegraphing with a sensual allure that kicked every hormone in Rafe's body into immediate overdrive.

He stared at the display, stunned. Fascinated. Awed by the artistry of light and shadow, tint and texture.

Then he opened the right panel, and awe accelerated into fury. More photographs filled this half of the board. All had been defaced. Some bore slashing *X*s across the subject. Others had expletives scrawled across the entire print. One in particular drew Rafe's eyes. According to the inscription that obliterated Allie's impish grin, only a fool would love this face—or buy the cosmetics she was peddling to the masses.

Rafe was still staring at the photograph when he heard the door to the processing unit open. Turning, he saw one of Avendez's assistants step inside.

Philips, Rafe recalled instantly. Jerry Philips. A student at the University of Texas, doing a summer photography internship with Avendez. The kid seemed to go out of his way to add to his image of a geek, Rafe thought. Thin, stoop-shouldered and nervous, he invariably dressed in baggy knee-length shorts, a burnt-orange UT sweatshirt several sizes too large and a ball cap. He jumped like a scalded cat whenever the Zebra shouted at him, which occurred frequently, and stammered almost incoherently every time Allie tried to put him at his ease.

When he saw Rafe in the center, he almost stopped short. "Wh-what are you doing in here?"

"Looking around."

"Uh, Mr. Avendez doesn't like people in here without his permission."

"I don't need his permission," Rafe returned easily.

"Oh." Philips stared at him for a few moments before belatedly remembering his mission. "I have to get some film."

Rafe stood aside while the assistant hurried past and fumbled a key into one of the locked, climate-controlled supply cabinets. He pulled out a tray of sealed foil packages and was heading for the door when Rafe nodded toward the montage of photos.

"This is quite a display. Did you help put it together?"

The kid's eyes skimmed over the array. "No, Mr. Avendez did it. He mounts the shots he particularly likes or dislikes, then studies them. When he's in the mood, he'll tell us what's right or wrong in the composition."

Rafe tapped a knuckle against the shot with the impish grin. "Did he tell you what was wrong with this one?"

"He didn't have to," the intern replied with a shrug. "Any first-year photography student would know we held the reflector at the wrong angle. The sunlight's too harsh on her face."

Shifting the tray to one hand, he swiped the back of his hand across his runny nose and studied the shot with critical eyes. "If I'd been setting up the shot, I would've used a polarizer to soften the background a little. Focus more on her mouth. God, what a mouth."

Rafe's eyes narrowed at the husky, reverent quality of the last few words. It appeared he could add the intern to the ever-expanding collection of males in love, or at least in lust, with Allie. The Viking, the Zebra, the Cigar, and now the Geek.

Turning over the possible implications in his mind, Rafe surveyed the kid. Correction, the man. For all his baggy shorts and stooped shoulders, Philips had to be in his mid-twenties. What was more, he had access to the processing unit...and to the mobile phone.

"Well, I gotta get this film to Mr. Avendez. Later, man."

"Later," Rafe replied.

He let himself out a few moments later and detoured to his casita to make a quick call. He'd already advised the NYPD detective handling Allie's case of the early-morning call. Now he'd put him to work on a specific phone number.

The detective promised to track down the mobile phone service and check its records for this particular number. It might take a few days, he warned. The explosion of cellular phones and the deregulation of the telephone companies had complicated the process considerably.

His mouth grim, Rafe rejoined the shoot. The spectacular sunrise, now more blue-and-gold than purple-and-red, didn't even warrant a passing glance. His total focus was on the woman draped in black and on the man with the half head of flowing black hair who crouched before her, his face obscured by a camera.

Last night's call could have come from anywhere—or from just a few yards away. It could have been made by anyone—or by Avendez, or his intern, or any one of the two dozen people who swarmed in and out of the processing center all day. Until he heard back from the police, Rafe was just speculating. Yet he knew he had to tell Allie about his suspicions. He also knew she wasn't going to like them.

Not wanting to disturb her during the shoot, he waited until the crew returned, dusty and tired from a long, exhausting day. Rafe grabbed a quick shower, then walked the short distance to her casita, only to discover that she wasn't there.

None of the crew members he questioned, Avendez included, knew where she was.

Eight

Using the low-frequency signals emitted by the beeper, Rafe located Allie in less than fifteen minutes.

Afterward, when he could view that quarter hour with some degree of calm and objectivity, he'd admit that his reaction when he found her might have been a bit extreme. At the time, however, he was driven only by a gut-wrenching fear.

The tenuous emotional distance he'd managed to keep between himself and his client vanished during the search. Mouth grim, stomach coiled in a tight knot, heart pounding a staccato, rapid-fire beat, he followed the signals to the resort's main building.

He found Allie in a small alcove just off the lobby. In the arms of a tall, dark-haired executive type with a wolfish grin on his too-handsome face that made Rafe want to take him out. Immediately. Painfully.

Blithely unaware of the hell she'd just put him through, Allie turned at the sound of his approach. Sliding an arm around the Executive's waist, she smiled a welcome.

"Rafe! You got my message."

"No, Miss Fortune, I didn't."

Her smile slipped at his low, fury-laced reply.

"But—but I called you," she protested. "When you didn't answer your phone, I left a voice mail."

"Try again. There wasn't any message on my phone."

She stiffened at his sneer. After a quick glance at the man beside her, she answered in a cool voice that only served to fan Rafe's anger.

"We'll talk about the mix-up later. Right now, I want to—"

"We'll talk about it now. In your casita. If your *friend* will excuse us."

"I don't think so," the man drawled.

The lazy smile and striped silk tie didn't fool Rafe for a second. He recognized another predator when he saw one. Holding the stranger's eyes with his own, he issued Allie a low warning.

"You'd better be careful. This one's not going to be as easy to handle as your other collectibles."

She stepped out of the man's hold, frowning. "What collectibles?"

"The Viking and the Zebra, not to mention El Tampico and the poor Geek."

"El Who? What on earth are you talking about?"

"I'm talking about this habit you have of conveniently dispensing with our agreement whenever you decide to take another stroll."

Anger flared in her brown eyes. "I see," she said tightly. "You know, Stone, I'm beginning to think this little talk you're insisting on is overdue."

"Way overdue," he concurred. "We'll finish this conversation at your casita."

"Oh, we'll finish it," she promised. "We'll finish a number of things. Before we go, though, I'd like to introduce you to Michael. Michael Fortune. My cousin," she added with false, dripping sweetness. "He stopped by on his way to L.A. to bring me some... paperwork."

In a more civilized mood, Rafe might have acknowledged his mistake with some semblance of grace. His ear might have registered Allie's brief hesitation, and wondered about this paperwork the Executive had delivered. At that moment, however, the fear that had gripped him when he found her missing was still too potent, too raw.

The best he could manage was a curt nod. "Fortune."

"Excuse me, Michael," Allie said, her voice low and taut. "I want to have a chat with my bodyguard. I'll call you later."

Much later, Rafe thought grimly as he escorted her across the tiled vestibule. There were a few things he and Allison Fortune had to get straight between them once and for all.

Much later, Allie thought as they stepped through the doors and the high desert twilight wrapped around them. They had a few things to sort out between them first, like the reasons behind Rafe's barely leashed anger. Her mind raced with a dozen explanations for his fury and rejected all but two.

He was upset, to put it mildly, over what he saw as a breech of his precious rules.

And he was jealous. Of Michael and this El Something and an unknown person otherwise known as the Geek. The idea stunned her, and angered her, and secretly thrilled her just a little. Having recently suffered a bout of the same malady herself, Allie recognized the symptoms. She slanted him a quick upward glance, taking in the tight line of his jaw and the glitter of suppressed fury in his eyes.

Her pulse raced. He was close, so close, to losing his iron-willed control. The thought sent little tingles of excitement racing through her blood. According to the background brief Michael had hand-delivered, Rafe Stone wasn't the kind of man to lose control very often. Her heart hammering, Allie wished she'd had time to do more than just skim the report. The little she'd read had provided a tantalizing glimpse into his background.

Rafael Alexander Stone. Born thirty years ago in Miami. Father a dock worker. Mother a Cuban immigrant. "Encouraged" to join the army as a teenager by an irate judge. One hitch, Special Forces, then started free-lancing. Specialty hostage extraction. Severely injured in a bomb blast several years ago. Parents now deceased. Subject divorced.

Allie wanted to know more about the man who'd taken such possession of her mind. A lot more. She intended to, before this night was over. First, though, they had to settle this business of the missing message.

Deciding to take the offensive, she swept into the casita and went right to the phone. She had the operator on the line before Rafe had slammed the door behind him.

"This is Allison Fortune. I left a voice mail for Mr. Rafe Stone earlier. I understand he didn't receive it. Would you tell me why, please?"

She listened for a moment, then nodded. "I see. Mr. Stone's here with me now. Would you repeat that to him, please."

She held out the phone, a challenge in her eyes. Rafe took it without a word, identified himself, and listened to the operator's apologetic explanation. The computerized voice mail system had gone down for an hour, but was back up now, and yes, Mr. Stone had a message from Miss Fortune waiting in the queue for him.

"This doesn't change a damn thing," he said shortly, hanging up. "The fact remains that I didn't get it."

"That wasn't my fault," Allie retorted, refusing to back down. Her eyes flicked over his still-damp hair. "You must have been in the shower when I called. Or maybe you had stepped out. Was that it, Rafe? Were you taking a little stroll, enjoying the sunset with someone? As you're so fond of accusing me of doing?"

He acknowledged her hit with an angry glare. For a moment, Allie thought he would deny his earlier, unflattering accusation. Then he expelled a harsh breath and shoved a hand through his hair.

"I guess I was wrong about that."

"Yes, you were," she replied, not yielding an inch. Her belligerence brought an apology of sorts.

"All right," he conceded with obvious reluctance. "Maybe I've been wrong about a number of things where you're concerned."

Allie had never considered herself the kind of person to make someone grovel, but she wasn't ready to let Rafe off the hook yet. Not when he was looking at her with that combination of irritation and frustration and something she couldn't quite define. It might have been grudging respect. Or admiration.

She didn't want admiration. Not from him. She wanted what her body had ached for ever since he'd cushioned her fall and held her in his arms and kissed her. What she'd wanted desperately last night, when he soothed her fears and ignited a need in her that had flared into liquid heat whenever she caught sight of him today.

His need was as great as her own. She knew it, wanted him to acknowledge it. Stepping closer, she pressed for more.

"What else were you wrong about? What do you think you know about me?"

His eyes skimmed her face, so close now to his own.

"What, Rafe?"

"I know you're a professional in the true sense of the word," he admitted. "You organize your time and yourself so you never keep the team waiting."

That was a start, but not exactly what Allie was looking for. "What else?"

"I've learned not to mistake your patience for passivity," he said slowly. "You keep your temper when Avendez tears everyone else's to shreds, and manage to direct him far more than he directs you. You're the one who drives the shoot, Allie. You make things happen without seeming to."

That surprised her a bit. Only Rocky and Kate had ever really grasped how often the quiet, seemingly docile Allie instigated events. To this day, Rocky blamed her twin for ninety-nine percent of the hours they'd spent in their room as punishment for some prank or another. The idea that Rafe had seen past Allie's outer shell and glimpsed the person within stirred an aching hope in her.

"And?" she asked, a little breathless now.

His mouth twisted. He lifted his hand, so slowly that Allie thought it would never reach its goal, and cupped her chin. "And, Miss Fortune, you've been driving me, as well. To near distraction."

Her heart gave a funny little lurch, displacing the last of her anger and indignation. This was better, she thought. Much better.

"I've been a little...distracted myself," she confessed, her fingers coming up to cup his. His hand felt so warm, so solid, layered as it was between her palm and her chin.

Rafe knew he should cut this discussion off. Every instinct in his body told him to put some distance between them, to drop his hand and step back.

He might have managed it, if her skin hadn't felt as smooth and soft as he remembered from last night. If her eyes hadn't cajoled and mesmerized and seduced him.

"What else Rafe?" she asked softly. "What else have you seen?"

"I've seen a woman of strength and generosity and humor, who can also be stubborn as hell and a real pain at times."

"All that, huh?"

Rafe had to put this conversation in perspective before it spiraled completely out of control and took them both with it. "You're my client, Allie. It's my job to observe you. To understand what makes you tick."

"Oh, no," she breathed, trapping his fingers with her own when he tried to tug them away. "You're not getting away with that one. What's between us now has nothing to do with clients or bodyguards or any business arrangements."

"A business arrangement is all that's between us."

"Is that so? What about this?" Turning her head, she pressed her lips against his palm.

"Allie . . ."

"Or this?" Her tongue stroked his skin.

Rafe yanked his hand away and stepped back. "This isn't smart."

"You know," she said on a little puff of exasperation, "I'm not the only one around here who can be stubborn as hell and a real pain at times."

Closing the small space between them, she wrapped both arms around his neck and dragged his mouth down to hers.

Rafe held himself rigid under her determined attack. He kept his hands at his side. He didn't allow his mouth to mold to hers. He thought of all the reasons this was wrong. All the reasons this violated his own unwritten professional code of conduct, not to mention the hard, painful lessons of his past. Then she opened her mouth under his, and he stopped thinking of anything but Allie.

At the touch of her tongue, the hunger he'd held in check since the night he'd met her exploded. One arm banded her waist, dragging her up against his chest while he took what she offered. Her breasts pressed against him urgently as she strained to give more, and more. Rafe took it all. Her kisses. Her fevered explorations with her mouth and hands and hips against his. Her breathless moan when he tugged her blouse loose with one hand and brought her nipple to turgid, pebbled hardness.

When he tumbled her to the bed some time later, she was stripped of everything but a pair of bikini panties that rode high on her hips. Rafe stood beside the bed, his hands on the snap of his jeans. His shirt had been

discarded, along with most of her clothes, during the
sensual dance that had brought them into the bedroom.

As he gazed down at her, his hand stilled. The bedroom lights were off, leaving only the dim glow from
the sitting room to pearl her skin. Her mouth was
swollen and red from his. Her breasts had peaked under his hands.

She was so beautiful. So damned beautiful.

Allie groaned at his hesitation. "If you tell me again
this is dumb or against your professional ethics or
some such nonsense, I'm going to... to do something
very unprofessional."

Rafe couldn't help himself. Eyes gleaming, he
planted his hands on his hips. "Oh, yeah? Like
what?"

She angled her head to gauge the degree of his resistance. Then she curled her legs under her and got to
her knees. Brushing his hands aside, she took possession of his zipper.

"Like this, Rafe."

The metal tab inched down, prong by prong. His
stomach hollowed at the touch of her lips against his
skin.

"Mmm..." she murmured, nuzzling the dark hair
swirling around his belly button. "Nice. And so deli-
ciously unethical. So unsmart."

The tab reached the bottom of the zipper. Palming
his hips, she slid his jeans over his flanks. All the
while, her mouth hovered inches from his skin. The

moist heat of her breath came through his cotton Jockey shorts like a warm, curling mist.

"Still being stubborn?" She hooked her hands in the waistband of his shorts.

Rafe didn't think he could get any harder. He was wrong. When her mouth brushed against his straining flesh, he knew he'd never wanted a woman as much as he wanted Allie. With a groan, he buried both hands in her hair and tilted her face up to his. Planting a knee on the bed beside her, he covered her mouth with his. She went boneless beneath his assault, and they fell back to the sheets.

Within moments, Allie was lost in a panting, straining world of pure sensation. Rafe's mouth held hers captive while his knee pried hers apart. His hands shaped and stroked and invaded her. She heard the rasp of her breath against his, felt the slickness of her inner flesh as he brought her to aching, greedy readiness. She clutched at him, moaning a soft protest when he eased aside for a few moments to sheathe himself, then opened eagerly for his entry.

She arched under him, meeting his every thrust with one of her own. His hands anchored her head for a kiss that left her spinning. Her body tightened around him, her muscles clenching rhythmically.

It might have been moments, or maybe it was hours, before he reached down between their sweat-slick bodies and found her center. Allie's fingers clutched frantically at his shoulders as he stroked her. A far corner of her mind registered the coiled, straining muscles of one shoulder, the ridges on the other. Then her world splintered into white-hot shards of pure sensation.

He climaxed not long after her. Driving into her with all the force of his powerful thighs, he left Allie shuddering with pleasure.

Gradually the thunder in Allie's ears receded. Slowly, the harsh rasp of Rafe's breathing softened. He rolled to his side, taking her with him, and she found the same warm notch between neck and shoulder she'd discovered last night.

She felt boneless. And slightly stunned. And wonderful.

Rafe, she noted when she opened her eyes some time later, didn't appear to share her wonder. The shadows in the bedroom had darkened during their fevered ballet. Just enough light spilled in from the sitting room for her to catch his frown.

"Don't you dare say this was dumb," she warned, in a voice still husky from passion.

"I won't. But it does . . . complicate things."

Allie fought a little niggle of hurt at the note of reserve in his voice. She was still tingling from head to toe, and it sounded as though he were already regretting the explosive passion they'd just shared.

"It doesn't have to complicate anything," she said, managing a weak smile. "Just because I jumped your bones tonight that doesn't mean I'll lose all control. We can take this slowly, Rafe. Or try to."

He brushed a strand of hair from her flushed, perspiration-sheened face. "Don't kid yourself. I wanted you to jump my bones. Or anything else you had a mind to. Badly."

"So what's the problem?"

Rafe hesitated. He didn't want to lay his unfounded suspicions on her, but he knew she wouldn't accept half truths or evasions. Any more than he could offer them. Not now. Not after what they'd just shared.

"The problem is last night's call," he said softly, easing out of the bed. "It bothered me."

Allie scooted up, pulling the sheet with her. She crossed her arms under her breasts, and Rafe dragged his hungry gaze from the plumped-up slopes.

"Well, it didn't exactly thrill me," she replied.

"I know, sweetheart."

The endearment came out before he could stop it. Cursing himself for the slip, Rafe groped for his shorts. He hadn't lied to Allie. The mind-blowing passion he'd just experienced complicated the hell out of things. His instincts told him he'd need every one of his senses on full alert for the next few days. He couldn't lose himself in Allie, and possibly lose her, as well. Following a faint trail of golden light, he located his jeans and stepped into them.

"Tell me again the pitch of the caller's voice," he ordered.

A ripple of unease crossed her face, robbing it of its rosy flush. Regret lanced through Rafe like a sharp dagger at its loss, but he persisted.

"Describe the caller's voice to me, Allie."

"Low and whispery," she answered reluctantly. "And sort of draggy, almost as though he was speaking in slow motion. And...and he always calls me Allison."

"The police suspect he's using a synthesizer to disguise his voice."

"Why would he need to disguise his—?" Her words died as she understood the answer to her own question. "Oh, my God! Do they think the caller might not be some obsessed fan? That someone I know could be making these calls?"

"It's possible."

Her fingers clutched the sheet. "But who?"

"Someone who wants to frighten you. Someone who's so obsessed with you, he wants to control you through these calls. Someone like Avendez," he suggested, anticipating her reaction.

It came with hurricane force. She jerked upright in the bed, her eyes flashing. "No way! Not Dom!"

"Why not? He's in love with you, Allie. Has been for a long while, I'd guess."

She shagged a hand through her hair. "For heaven's sake, I know that. We've talked about it. Many times. But I can't give him what he needs, and we've both agreed not to let it destroy our friendship."

Rafe shook his head. "You can't be friends with a man who's in love with you."

"Yes, I can," she argued stubbornly. "Especially with a man who's in love with me. I don't have that many friends, Rafe. This business doesn't allow it. I'm not going to abandon one I trust and admire."

"It doesn't work that way, Allie. No man is content with just friendship from a woman he lusts for."

Her head snapped back. "Lusts for?"

"You said yourself he was in love with you."

She didn't answer for a moment. When she did, her voice was low and strained. "Not everyone equates love with lust."

Rafe reached for the light switch, aware of the need to see her face while he negotiated this dangerous turn in the conversation.

"You're a beautiful woman," he told her, choosing his words with great care. "The kind who can mix a man up. Mix him up so much he could confuse lust with love. Friendship with obsession."

Her brown eyes stared up at him for long moments. Rafe cursed himself for the doubt he saw in them.

"Do I confuse you, Rafe?" she asked in a quiet voice.

He couldn't give her anything but the truth. "You confuse the hell out of me."

"I see."

He ached to take her in his arms. To stop the retreat he saw in her eyes before it became a full rout. He curled his hands into fists to keep from reaching for her.

Hurt washed through Allie in tiny, lapping waves. She couldn't believe Rafe thought the soaring passion they'd shared was mere animal lust. At this point, she wasn't quite sure what it was. Right now, she wasn't sure she cared.

"I'm not saying Avendez made those calls," he said. "Just that it's a possibility."

Allie listened mutely while he related his request to have the police check the records of the mobile phone in the processing unit. A hard lump formed in her throat as he mentioned his reservations about the other members of the crew, including the gangly intern.

"I know these people," she said tightly. "I can't believe any of one them is so...so obsessed with me that he'd want to hurt me."

"Just keep your eyes open, okay? And the beeper with you."

Allie nodded, unable to speak around the lump in her throat.

"Get dressed, and I'll take you back to dinner," he said quietly.

Only moments ago, she'd felt replete and relaxed and wonderful. Now, she wanted Rafe out of her room before she did something stupid, like crying. In tight silence, she watched as he bent to snag his shirt from the floor.

Seeing his full torso in the light for the first time, Allie couldn't prevent a startled gasp. The scars that disfigured one side of his chin and neck continued over his shoulder and made a tortured moonscape of his back.

At the sound of her shock, Rafe froze. Then he shrugged into his shirt and turned, his fingers working the buttons. "I'll wait for you in the sitting room."

"Wait!" Furious with herself for her unguarded response, Allie scrambled off the bed, dragging the sheet with her. "Rafe, I'm sorry. It's just that your back... It must have..."

She reached out to touch him, her own hurt swamped by an awareness of the anguish he must have suffered.

He caught her hand and held it away. "It's okay, Allie. I'm used to that kind of reaction."

Nine

After a strained dinner with Michael and Rafe, followed by an endless night of tossing and turning, Allie woke hollow-eyed and irritable the next morning. Even a hard, driving run through a colorful dawn couldn't clear her sluggish mind.

Every time she thought of the possibility that someone on the crew could have been making the calls, she felt a little sick.

And every time she tried to make sense of those moments in Rafe's arms, he distracted her. She could hear his rasping breath as he paced her. See the gray sweats plastered against his chest and his pumping thighs from the corner of her eye. Remember the feel of those thighs against hers as he brought her to a shattering climax. Whenever Allie contrasted their breathless passion with Rafe's subsequent withdrawal, she grew angry all over again. And hurt. And confused.

Whenever she replayed that first startling glimpse of his back in her mind and heard her dismayed gasp, she berated herself. It had been obvious from the way Rafe drew away from her touch that his scars went deeper than the surface disfigurement. How deep, she didn't know. She wasn't sure he did, either.

She was still struggling with these conflicting, draining emotions when the crew piled into rented vehicles and drove into the mountains, to the site of the day's shoot. Even surrounded by tall stands of pine and whispering aspen groves, she couldn't clear her mind and concentrate on her work.

Rafe's suspicions of Dom plagued her. Throughout the shoot, her muscles felt still and uncoordinated, and her thoughts wandered down paths that made her tense with worry.

"Allie, for God's sake!" the photographer snarled after three frustrating hours. "You're supposed to be enjoying your little walk through these trees! It's hard enough to shoot in this shifting light, without you looking like you just stepped in a pile of fresh deer poop. What's with you this morning?"

"Nothing," she murmured.

"Well, loosen up." He bent over the camera. "Lift your chin. Give me some teeth. *Some,* I said!"

Allie tilted her face to the canopy formed by the silver-barked aspens. Glittering green leaves with just a hint of gold to herald the frosts to come fluttered in the morning breeze. Sunlight filtered through the branches and dappled her face.

"Hold it," Dom ordered. "Hold it. Now tilt your head back. More. More."

The crisp mountain air should have cleared her mind, but it didn't. The sharp tang of pine resin should have replaced the lingering scent of Rafe's skin, yet she carried its essence with her. The rough bark under her fingertips should have erased the remembered feel of the ridged scars. Instead, the scaly bark only served to remind her of what he must have suffered. Her face tightened in sympathy.

"Dammit!" Dom stalked to her side, dried leaves crunching under his foot with each angry step. "What the hell's going on here?"

Allie twisted her neck a little to ease the aching muscles. "Nothing."

He glared at her. "You've been stiff as a board this morning."

She tried to summon up the energy to soothe his ragged temper, and failed. "Sorry," she returned shortly.

A flush stained his neck at her unaccustomed curtness. "I want your head back. Back, dammit!"

Splaying his fingers through her hair, he yanked her head to the required angle. Their wills clashed, and for an instant, treacherous doubt snaked through Allie's mind. Was this just another display of Dom's infamous temper? Or was there something more, something darker, behind the heat in his eyes?

"Take your hands off her, Avendez."

Dom slewed around, his face a mask of fury. "Butt out, Stone. This isn't any of your business."

"Wrong. She is my business."

Allie might have been grateful for Rafe's intervention, if his words hadn't brought memories of last night crashing down on her once more. He'd warned her then that a business arrangement was all that bound them. She should have listened, she told herself bitterly. She darn well should have listened. If she had, maybe she wouldn't be having these awful doubts about herself and Rafe and a man who'd been her friend longer than she could remember.

"It's all right," she snapped, earning a hard look from both men.

Allie could count on the fingers of one hand the number of times she'd lost her poise during a shoot. If she didn't get herself under control, this might be one of them.

"We've got a lot to do today and tonight," she said, in a more even tone. "Let's just get on with it."

As the day wore on, Dom's temper went from bad to worse. The tension took its toll on everyone, from the equipment handlers to the art director, who stalked off in a huff when Dom informed him he wouldn't recognize an effective layout if it jumped up and took a chunk out of his ass. When their rented vehicles finally drove through the gates of Rancho Tremayo an hour before dusk, Allie might have wept with relief if she didn't know she would soon be heading back out again. This time in velvet and pearls.

Of all the nights to shoot against the backdrop of a gala benefit performance at the Santa Fe Opera, she thought wearily. She felt about as gay and glamorous as a lump of uncooked cookie dough.

* * *

Rafe tugged at his black satin bow tie as he crossed to Allie's casita. Of all the nights to have to rig himself out in a rented tux and starched white shirt, he thought savagely. He was tired, edgy, and frustrated by the fact that the NYPD detective working Allie's case had come down with the flu and no one else in the damned department knew anything about a record of calls from the mobile phone.

Even worse, he'd had to struggle all day to keep his mind on his client's security and off their moments locked in each other's arms last night. Despite his every effort to suppress it, Rafe's need for the woman had grown with every passing hour. After a long, sleepless night and a morning of watching her move with deliberate grace among the trees, he'd ached with the urge to drag Allie away from the crew, lay her down in the lush meadow grass and make love to her under the endless blue sky.

By late afternoon, however, his desire had shifted focus. Then, Rafe had wanted only to drag her away from the crew and lay her down and watch her drift into sleep. She desperately needed rest, yet she pushed herself even harder than the Zebra pushed her. It had been hard enough on Rafe to stand on the sidelines while Avendez savaged her all day. Now he had to watch the entire process repeat itself tonight.

If the woman who opened the door to him a few moments later felt drained or fatigued, however, she didn't show it. She looked composed and in control and so elegant that Rafe's stomach twisted up in a bow to match his tie.

By now, he knew enough about her profession to recognize the hallmarks of the trade. A master stylist had swept her hair up in a mass of loose curls. Skillful shading added dramatic emphasis to her eyes and full mouth. The black velvet gown that hugged her slender figure like a glove had to have come from a designer's private collection.

Yet as Rafe waited for the ground to steady under him, he decided that Allie didn't owe her innate elegance to any outside factors. It was more a matter of personal style. The way she carried herself. Her grace under constant, unrelenting pressure. As if to prove the validity of his assessment, she smiled through the strain that had hovered between them since last night.

"Nice tie."

"Don't get too used to it," he warned, following her lead. "I've got the other one in my pocket."

One delicate brow rose as he took her cloak. "You do? Why?"

"It's my version of American Express," he replied, settling the heavy velvet around her shoulders. "I never leave home without it."

She angled her head, surprise sculpting her face as she glanced up at him. "What is it, a lucky charm?"

"More or less."

"Funny," she murmured, her eyes holding his. "I wouldn't have thought of you as superstitious. I guess

I have as much to learn about you as you do about me."

"Allie..."

"We need to talk, Rafe," she said quietly. "About what happened last night."

"I know."

"Tonight? After the opera?"

"Maybe. If you're not too tired."

And if he could manage to keep his hands off her. At this moment, that possibility seemed remote. Her scent surrounded him, delicate and floral and more erotic than anything he could remember on a woman. His body hardened, and he ached to draw her back, to feel her length pressed to his. Shoving the urge to the distant corner of his mind where it belonged, he offered her his arm.

She hesitated, then slid her hand into the bend of his elbow. Rafe's muscles quivered involuntarily at her touch.

"Let's hope your lucky charm works tonight," she said, a touch of weariness creeping into her voice, despite her brave front. "Maybe we'll wrap this sequence up early and actually get to enjoy ourselves at the opera."

Rafe figured his enjoyment meter would peg out about two and a half minutes after the curtain went up. But if an evening of music would ease some of the strain on Allie's shoulders, he'd sit through a half-dozen performances.

* * *

They arrived at the dramatic open-air theater on the outskirts of Santa Fe to find the advance crew already on the scene. After some consultation and a good many expletives, Avendez decided to shoot the first sequence using the sweeping arch of the half roof over the stage and the orchestra pit as a backdrop. The composition, he announced, would center Allie's face and black dress against the golden lights of the arch, which thrust like a ship's prow into the night. Black on gold on black was how he described it. Simple. Dramatic. Stunning.

This simple shot, Rafe knew by now, would require half a ton of equipment. Metal rasped against metal as Avendez's assistants worked feverishly to mount huge box strobes on the portable scaffolding. The generator hummed a steady counterpoint to the murmur of the crowd, many of whom wandered over to watch, champagne glasses in hand.

Rafe's jaw tightened as he scanned the milling crowd. Dressed in everything from formal evening wear to the distinctive Santa Fe look that only its residents could carry off, they added to the bustle and confusion around the shoot.

The gawkers were crowding too close for his comfort. Mingling with the crew. Observing while Dom positioned Allie and ran some test Polaroids. Eyes narrowed, nerves tight, Rafe moved through the chattering throng to the uniformed officer the Santa Fe police had provided at his request.

The officer must have sensed Rafe's tension. She frowned slightly, studying his expression. "Everything all right, Mr. Stone?"

He hesitated, then gave the only answer he could. "It doesn't feel right."

She nodded and hitched her Sam Browne belt a little higher on her hips. "I'll keep my eyes open."

Unease nagged at Rafe as he swept the scene. "I wish I could tell you what to look for."

"I wish you could, too," she answered with a grin.

Rafe drifted through the crowd, studying faces and hands and shoes, looking for something that didn't belong, didn't fit. He couldn't pinpoint the source of his tension, unless it was the sense of suppressed excitement that shimmered in the night air. Maybe the excitement was caused by the gala event. Maybe by the added novelty of the shoot. Whatever generated this electric air, Rafe didn't like it.

Even when Dom yelled for quiet and began his ritual dance with Allie, talk fluttered around the edges of the shoot. People drifted in and out of the circle of onlookers. A well-dressed matron stumbled over the thick cables snaking from the generator.

Idly Rafe followed the lines of cabling from the generator to the scaffolding that supported the strobes. As he scanned the bank of overhead lights, one of them dipped and tilted at an odd angle. Suddenly Rafe tasted danger. He shoved his way past indignant spectators and started toward Allie.

At that precise moment, Avendez jerked his head up from the viewfinder, his lips curled back in a snarl. "Who's messing with the lighting? What the hell's—? Jesus!"

The snap of a cable whipping loose sounded over the noise of the crowd.

A wild arc of light skewered the night, then swept the sky at a crazy angle.

Someone screamed.

Rafe didn't need to look up to know one of the huge box strobes had broken loose from the scaffolding and was now swinging wildly at the end of its anchoring line. Bright light flashed into his eyes, momentarily blinding him, then arced away. Black spots obscured his vision as he pushed through the crowd.

"Allie!" Avendez shouted in panic. His camera shattered when he threw it aside and raced toward her. "Move! Get the hell out of the way!"

Blinded by the dazzling light, Allie threw an arm up over her eyes and tried to sidestep through the forest of cables and reflectors caging her. The strobe swung toward her in a deadly arc.

Rafe reached her a half second before the huge box hit the bottom of its vicious swing. Wrapping an arm around her waist, he spun around and yanked her out of its path. A corner of the strobe struck him a glancing blow on the shoulder. He felt a sharp metal edge slice through his tux like a razor, but his only concern at that moment was for Allie.

Banding her against his side to shield her from the backswing, he shoved his way through the equipment. Behind him, reflectors crashed as the strobe knocked them from their stands. He heard Avendez shouting from the other side of the slashing arc, but ignored him.

Setting Allie on her feet, he steadied her with hard hands on her upper arms. "Are you all right?"

Her eyes were huge pools of shock in a chalk-white face. She opened her mouth. No sound came out.

"Allie, sweetheart, are you hurt?"

"N-no."

At the small squeak, Rafe groaned and folded her in his arms again.

"Allie!" Avendez's hoarse shout sounded behind them.

Twisting his head, Rafe saw the photographer grab for the swinging strobe and wrestle it to a stop. Then he pushed it aside and pounded toward them.

Reluctantly Rafe loosened his hold. A shaken Allie stepped out of his arms. Avendez was at her side the next instant. Looping an arm around her neck, he dragged her into a fierce hug.

The naked fear on his face was the only thing that kept Rafe from reaching out and ripping the man's arm off at the shoulder socket.

"God, Allie, you scared the crap out of me!" The photographer's voice shook as he buried his face in her hair.

She gave a weak, muffled laugh and disengaged herself. "I didn't do it on purpose."

"Yeah, right. Some models will do anything to get a little extra attention." He searched her face, his own anxious. "You sure you're okay?"

Gently she brushed a strand of black hair from the side of his face. "I'm fine, Dom."

Rafe stood back, observing the scene with a surge of conflicting emotions. Part of him wanted to step between them, to jerk Allie's attention away from Avendez and back to him. Another part admired her loyalty to a man she claimed as friend.

Reluctantly Rafe moved the photographer to the bottom of his list of potential late-night callers. The man hadn't been able to hide the fear that twisted through him a few moments ago, or the love he tried to disguise behind his gruff manner.

A small movement to his side caught Rafe's attention. He wasn't the only one observing the scene between photographer and model. Xola gripped Allie's cloak in both hands, her eyes bleak. The rest of the crew crowded behind her. Dom's senior assistant stood white-faced, while the knobby-kneed Geek clutched a crumpled reflector in both hands.

Then another figure snagged Rafe's attention. Easing his way through the crew, he reached the police officer's side.

"I thought you might be interested in this, Mr. Stone."

Using a handkerchief, she lifted the end of a thick, black cable. The rubber coating was serrated, the wires twisted.

"Looks to me like someone or something sawed through this cable," she murmured.

A muscle in Rafe's jaw twitched. "Looks that way to me, too. Can you get an evidence technician out here, fast?"

"I already called one. He's on his way."

It took almost an hour for the lab tech to arrive on the scene and collect the evidence. In private conversation with Rafe, he admitted that the chances of lifting a complete print from the porous rubber coating were pretty slim, but maybe the experts at the crime lab in Albuquerque could get enough points to make a positive ID.

In the meantime, the uniformed officer took statements from witnesses. No one, it turned out, had seen anything suspicious.

At that point, Rafe made an instant decision. Until the results of the police checks came in, he was getting Allie away from the crew and the shoot. And from the damn schedule that was driving her into the ground.

Stunned by the idea that the incident might not have been an accident, she made no protest when Rafe bundled her into the car. She'd recovered enough from her shock, however, to stammer a protest when he slammed the door to her casita behind them and told her brusquely to get changed and pack a bag.

"What?"

"Bring something warm."

She gaped at him. "Something warm?"

"We're getting out of here."

"Tonight?"

"Tonight. And we'll stay out until I get the answers to a few questions."

"But... but I can't just leave. The shoot... The schedule..."

"To hell with the schedule."

Rafe strode over to her and lifted her chin with a hard hand. "You promised to follow my orders if I perceived a threat to your safety. Immediately. Without question."

She opened her mouth, then closed it with a snap.

"You've got five minutes to get changed and packed, Allie. Then we're out of here."

Ten

Allie wedged a shoulder against the car door and studied the man beside her through half-lowered lashes.

In the glare of headlights, his profile appeared stark and uncompromising. A loose strand of dark hair brushed his forehead. His mouth was set in a hard line, and his chin jutted out to meet the night. He'd tugged off his bow tie and exchanged his tux for his sheepskin-lined vest during a quick stop at his casita, but he hadn't taken the time to change his white shirt or his dark slacks.

In the few moments he'd given her to get ready, Allie had traded her velvet gown for jeans and a soft, baggy gray turtleneck. Rafe had paced like a caged mountain lion while she hurriedly tossed a few things into her weekender. She'd snatched the case off the bed and started to hurry out, only to pause and scoop up the tin carousel at the last minute.

She held the small toy in her lap now, reluctant to set it in the back seat with the carryalls. Somehow it helped to have the keepsake within reach, as if Kate's carousel could somehow bestow on Allie a measure of her grandmother's indomitable strength in times of crisis.

No, not Kate's carousel, she remembered bleakly. Hers. Kate was dead...as Allie might be, if Rafe hadn't moved so quickly. Shivers danced all over her skin. She hunched lower in the seat and hugged her arms across her chest.

"Cold?" Rafe's deep voice cut through the darkness, steady and reassuring. He groped for the instrument panel. "Want some heat?"

"No," she replied.

Yes, her mind screamed.

Yes, she wanted some heat. His heat. More than she could ever remember wanting anything. She longed to curl into his arms and shut out the horror of the past hour. Pretend it had never happened. She ached for the passion, the release, the blessed mindlessness, that she'd found with him last night.

As much as she wanted him, though, she was determined not to shove aside his objections and push herself on him. Not again. Not after last night. He'd have to find his way to her this time. Allie only hoped he didn't take too long in the process.

"Where are we going?" she asked, needing the sound of his voice, if nothing else.

"To Devil's Peak."

"That tells me a lot."

He slanted her a small smile. "It's a ski lodge up in the mountains, about an hour from here."

"Why there?"

"From what I understand, the place is packed in winter, but pretty well deserted this time of year. I reserved a cabin while you were packing."

"How did you know about this place?"

"I made a few inquiries when we first got to Santa Fe. I always like to have an escape route and a rendezvous point predesignated."

"I see." Allie swallowed. "Did you...did you think something like this might happen?"

He gripped the wheel, his jaw squaring. "I considered it a possibility."

Shaken, Allie shrank back against the door. It was bad enough thinking someone she knew might be fixating on her because of a sick, twisted love. The idea that the same someone might be deliberately trying to maim or kill her frightened her far more.

No wonder he'd been so reluctant last night. She'd brushed aside his objections, pooh-poohed his professional concerns in her hunger for this man. Practically forced him to make love to her. She'd made light of his need to keep some distance between them so that he could maintain his alertness. She wouldn't make light of it again.

"Why?" she asked, feeling more than a little ill. "Why would someone who professes to...to love me want to hurt me?"

"Maybe it's not you he's out to hurt. A shrink might suggest he's using you to get at all the women who've hurt *him*. Or maybe," Rafe finished slowly, frowning at the road ahead, "he's trying to get at someone else through you."

Allie stared at him, her eyes widening. "Someone else? My parents, you mean?"

"Your parents," Rafe replied, his brow furrowed. "Or the entire Fortune family, as embodied by Fortune Cosmetics."

"You...you think he might be harassing me because I'm Fortune Cosmetics's new 'face'?"

"I don't know. I'm just guessing. When did these calls start? Before or after you agreed to do this ad campaign?"

Numbly Allie counted backward through the nights she'd been jerked from sleep.

"After," she whispered. "They started after my first meeting with Dom in New York to discuss the possibility of doing the shoot."

Rafe gripped the steering wheel. Avendez again. It always came back to Avendez. Yet the man had thrown himself at the strobe to stop its wild swing, sheet-white with fear for Allie. As much as Rafe would have loved to pin the calls on the vile-tempered photographer, it didn't feel right. Not after tonight.

Plenty of others had been present tonight, though. Xola, with her husky voice and her one-sided love for Avendez. The rest of the crew, including the Geek. Plus a whole new cast of opera-goers. Rafe could only hope that the lab in Albuquerque lifted some usable prints from that severed cable.

His mind churned with the possibilities, and it was some time before Rafe noticed that Allie was breathing deeply. She had wedged herself against the door and rested her head at an uncomfortable angle against the seat back. In the dim glow from the instrument panel, he could see the sweep of her black lashes against her cheek and a quick bobble as her chin dropped, then jerked upward again. She shook her head, as if to clear it and mumbled something. A few moments later, her chin dipped again.

Keeping one hand on the wheel, Rafe reached over and eased her into the circle of his arm. She gave a little sigh and burrowed her nose in the base of his neck. She went for that spot every time, he thought in mingled amusement and resignation.

He spent the rest of the long drive breathing in the faint, totally erotic scent of her hair and reliving his terror when the strobe light had swung toward her. Maybe he'd overreacted when he decided to yank her away from Rancho Tremayo, he conceded. Maybe the mobile phone and the cut cable had nothing to do with her late-night caller. But Rafe had gone beyond maybes where Allie was concerned.

Besides, he argued silently, she needed rest. Those killer marathon hours in front of the camera, piled on top of the calls, had taken more of a toll on her than she'd admit. Rafe had done his part, as well, adding to her stress by letting their relationship slip past the boundaries of employer and employee into something he couldn't quite define.

He couldn't sort through the problem of their ill-defined relationship, not while he was responsible for her safety. But he could damn well keep her under wraps and see that she got some rest until the police came up with some answers.

Allie woke to a dark room, a fuzzy mouth, and the sound of water running. Groggy and disoriented, she pushed herself up on one elbow. It took her a few moments to grasp that she was in a strange bed in an unfamiliar bedroom. Blinking, she stared at the contorted shadow dancing against the far wall. Gradually she realized that it came from the narrow slice of light spilling from the adjoining bathroom. A few seconds later, a low, muttered curse identified the shadow as Rafe.

Frowning, Allie slid out from under a plump down comforter. Cold air immediately raised goose bumps over her body. *All* over her body, except for the small patches of skin covered by her bikini panties and bra. She glanced down in confusion. She didn't remember climbing into bed, much less undressing.

Another muted exclamation from the bathroom made the question of how she'd gotten into bed irrelevant. Spotting her baggy gray sweater on a chair a few steps away from the bed, she dragged it on and padded barefoot across the smooth, pine-planked floor.

At first glance, she couldn't figure out what in the world Rafe was doing. He stood sideways at the sink, naked to the waist and twisted halfway around. His right arm reached over his shoulder, while his left gripped a plastic bottle.

Eyes wide, Allie skimmed her gaze down his long, lean torso. Twisted as they were, his chest muscles bunched and gleamed in the bright glow of the lights. His unbelted black dress pants rode low on his narrow hips. Allie had barely absorbed the impact of his raw masculinity when she noticed the white shirt stained with blood lying at his feet.

Shoving open the door, she stepped inside. "Rafe! What happened?"

He brought his head around. "Sorry," he muttered. "I didn't mean to wake you."

"Never mind me. What's the matter? Why are you bleeding?"

"I'm not, anymore."

Pushing her tangled hair out of her eyes, she stared at him in confusion. "But...what happened?"

"The strobe cut through my tux when it swung past and nicked the skin, that's all. Go back to bed. I'll be done here in a few minutes and won't disturb you anymore."

She didn't even dignify that with a reply. Taking the plastic bottle from his hand, she glanced down at the label.

"Do you always carry emergency medical supplies, as well as maintain an escape route and alternate... What was it?"

"Rendezvous point." He shook his head, grinning a little. "No. I got the antiseptic from the manager when I checked in. Go back to bed, Allie. I'm almost done."

"Turn around."

His grin faded. "I can manage."

"Turn around, Rafe."

He stared down at her for a moment, his blue eyes unreadable.

"Turn around," she ordered softly.

The tendons in his neck corded. For a moment, she thought he would refuse. Then he shifted so that the light fell on his back.

This time, Allie managed to control her gasp. Barely. The bloody slash across the ridged and puckered flesh of his shoulder was more than just a nick. Blood had smeared where Rafe had reached it, and crusted where he couldn't.

Grabbing a pad of folded toilet tissue, she splashed it with antiseptic and dabbed it on the gash. Rafe flinched at the sting, his muscles contracting involuntarily under the scarred flesh.

Frowning, Allie wiped away the dried blood. "This should be stitched."

"It's not that deep."

"How would you know?" she retorted. "You can't even see it."

He twisted his head to look over his shoulder. "It just needs cleaning."

"Hold still!"

Biting down on her lower lip, Allie folded a fresh pad and dabbed at the cut. The more she cleansed, the more she worried. She didn't know much about wounds, but this one looked like it needed suturing.

"I think we should get you to a doctor. This needs to be stitched, or it won't close properly. It could leave a—"

She broke off, flushing. To her infinite relief, his eyes held only a glimmer of wry amusement when he twisted around.

"It could leave a scar," she finished tartly. "*Another* scar, which you obviously don't need. Hold still and let me finish."

As she worked, the tension in the small room seemed to lessen by imperceptible degrees. Under her gentle hands, Rafe's back and shoulders lost some of their rigidity. For long moments, Allie focused only on the bloody gash and the sharp scent of antiseptic. Gradually the warmth of the skin under her fingertips nudged into her consciousness. Along with the sweep of Rafe's lean, powerful body. And the tiny arrow of dark hair at the small of his back. It disappeared into the loosened waistband of his slacks, Allie noted, wondering distractedly whether it followed his spine all the way down to the swell of his buttocks. He had tight, taut buns, she remembered suddenly. She'd gripped them last night, when . . .

"Are you finished?"

"What?"

He peered over his shoulder. "Are you done? It looks okay from here."

Dropping the folded pad in the john, she flushed it. "Well, the cut's crusted over and it's not bleeding, but I still think you should have a doctor look at it."

"Maybe later," he answered with a shrug, reaching for the bottle she held in one hand. While he screwed on the cap and cleaned up the sink, Allie brought down the toilet lid and perched on the seat. Drawing up her knees under her baggy sweater, she wrapped both arms around them.

"What caused the explosion, Rafe?" she asked, her voice quiet over the splash of water in the sink.

His hand stilled. "How do you know it was an explosion?"

"I asked Michael to run a background check on you," she replied, uncomfortable about admitting she'd invaded his privacy but beyond evasion. "He stopped by on his way to L.A. to deliver it."

"Your cousin struck me as an efficient type. Didn't his report include all the gory details?"

"No. Tell me. Please."

He twisted the tap to shut off the sluicing water. "Why, Allie? Why do you want to know?"

She wet her lips, a little unnerved by the hard demand in his eyes. "I want to know about you, Rafe. As much about you as you'll share with me. If I'm going to make any sense of last night..." She swallowed painfully. "If I'm going to know whether I'm confusing lust with... with something else, I need to understand you.''

Rafe stared down at her, battling an instinctive withdrawal. Over the years, he'd learned to field the sometimes prurient questions about his scars with a shrug or a cold stare. He couldn't shrug off Allie, though. There was no trace of morbid curiosity in the brown eyes that held his. She wanted to know about him, as much of him as he was willing to share.

He hadn't shared with anyone for a long time, Rafe realized. Too long. Still, reluctance tugged at him as he propped a bare foot on the edge of the tub and rested his elbows on his knee.

''I was bringing a client out of Central America,'' he said slowly, forcing each word past a solid wall of reticence. ''An oil-field exploration engineer who got caught in the middle of a nasty little revolution. The ruling junta thought he'd aided the rebels in the field. The guerrillas thought he'd betrayed the location of their headquarters to the *federalistas*. I never found out which side planted the bomb under the car.''

With a deliberate effort, Rafe blanked the shattering explosion, the leaping flames, the screams of the engineer he'd dragged from the wreckage, from his mind.

''At least the bombing caught the attention of the world press. The U.S. was able to pressure the junta into releasing us after a few unpleasant weeks in what passed for a hospital.''

"And when you got home?" Allie asked softly. "Couldn't the doctors do anything?"

Rafe lifted a shoulder. "The oil company paid for a whole team of plastic surgeons. After several skin grafts, and more time than I wanted to spend in hospitals, I decided I'd had enough."

So had his wife, Rafe remembered. His brief marriage, already shaky from his prolonged absences, hadn't survived the reconstruction period.

"Do they hurt?" Allie asked, her gaze gentle on the scars.

"The skin gets tight and pulls a little at times, but it doesn't hurt."

If someone had told Rafe that he'd be standing with one foot propped on the edge of a bathtub in the middle of the night, discussing his scars with a tousled-haired woman perched on a toilet seat, he would've snorted in derision. He hadn't talked about the bombing and its aftermath to anyone. Ever. He didn't like talking about it now.

Allie tilted her head. "Does massage help? I've got some lotion in my bag. I could rub it in, to keep the skin supple."

That was all he needed, Rafe thought. His body was still tight from the feel of Allie's hands on it once tonight. He didn't think he could handle another session, no matter how innocent.

"No, thanks," he replied, rising. "Not tonight."

Not any time in the foreseeable future, he resolved. The only way to get them through the next few days was to keep his hands off her and hers off him.

Her bare feet slid to the floor. "Are you sure? This is good stuff. Fortune Cosmetics's newest formula. Guaranteed to erase lines, drench dry cells, and generally take off ten years or so."

She stood close. Too close. Rafe caught a faint scent of the perfume that had tortured him all during the drive along the narrow, twisting mountain road.

"Not tonight. You need your sleep, remember? Eight hours minimum."

"Eight hours minimum...during a shoot." Her eyes clouded, and worry crept across her face. "How long do you think we'll be here?"

"Two days. Maybe three. Until I get some answers from the New York and Santa Fe police."

"We're supposed to wrap up here by the end of the week," she replied, worrying her lower lip with her teeth. "We've got studio time reserved in New York next week, and taping for TV spots scheduled the following week."

"They might have to be rescheduled."

"But Dom and the crew will just be wasting their—"

"Forget about Dom and the crew," Rafe said roughly. "Think about yourself for once."

She blinked, startled by his vehemence.

Rafe couldn't help himself. He violated the firm rule he'd just laid down for himself and brushed a thumb across the fragile skin above her cheeks.

"You won't be much good to Avendez with shadows under your eyes and worry etching lines in your face. Just relax for the next day or two. Give the police time to do their jobs."

Oh, sure, Allie thought. She was supposed to relax, with the entire crew twiddling their thumbs? With her father and Caroline and the entire Fortune clan waiting anxiously for the launch of the new line? With nothing to distract her from Rafe's constant presence?

Not hardly.

Rafe dropped his hand. "Get some sleep, Allie. I'll finish cleaning up in here."

Nodding, she opened the door and stepped out of the bathroom. Only then did she discover that the cabin contained exactly one other room.

She halted, her brows slanting as she stood in the middle of the floor and surveyed the spacious living/ sleeping area. Enough light streamed out of the bathroom for her to make out a stone fireplace against the far wall, a rustic-looking sofa and pair of chairs grouped in front of it, a table with two chairs beside the window, and the rumpled bed she'd crawled out of some moments before.

As her eyes became more accustomed to the shadows, she made out the shape of a folded blanket and pillow that had been tossed on the sofa. Obviously

Rafe planned to sleep there. Three yards away from her. In the same cabin.

And he imagined she was going to get some rest?

Shaking her head, she crossed to the queen-size bed. She had tucked her icy toes inside the down comforter and started to slide beneath its billowing warmth when a gleam of reflected light caught her eye.

Reaching out, she plucked the carousel off the bedside table. Unerringly her fingers wound it just the right number of times. When she set it down and released the key, the tinkling melody that had followed her into sleep as a child more times than she could count filled the night. Sighing, she snuggled into the depths of the covers.

On the other side of the bathroom door, Rafe froze, with one arm poking through the neck of a clean T-shirt. His tensed muscles slowly relaxed as he identified the sound that drifted to him.

He didn't recognize the song, although it sounded vaguely familiar. The tune was delicate, and hauntingly beautiful, like Allie. Classy... like Allie. Listening intently, Rafe shoved his other arm into the T-shirt.

He clicked off the bathroom light a few moments later and walked into the outer room, standing still until his eyes adjusted to the sudden darkness. While he waited, the song tinkled to a stop. In the quiet that followed, he made out the slow rise and fall of Allie's breathing.

Eleven

It should have been the perfect setting for a quiet, restful evening. A pine fire cackled in the stone fireplace. Patsy Cline crooned soulfully over the radio that constituted the sole form of electronic entertainment in the rustic cabin. The built-in shelves beside the fireplace had yielded a stack of old magazines, children's games, and a well-worn edition of Tom Clancy's first blockbuster novel.

Rafe stuck a finger in the paperback to mark his place and shot the woman pacing restlessly in front of the fire an exasperated look. He hadn't read two pages in the past hour. Hell, he hadn't read two pages all day. Allie smiling and serene was enough to make any man break out in a cold sweat. Allie impatient and in a snit could drive a saint to seriously consider ropes and chains and other forms of bondage.

Rafe had never claimed to be anything close to a saint.

"Allie, for Pete's sake. Will you please relax?"

She whirled, her hair a fan of dark auburn against the brighter red of the flames. "I can't. We've been here almost twenty-four hours. How long does it take to test for fingerprints or track down phone records?''

''I told you. The detective working the phone records was out with the flu. His partner's running them down now. And the Santa Fe police sent the cable housing to a special lab in Albuquerque. They promised to call with the results as soon as they get them.''

''And my father was satisfied with that? He didn't suggest he use his influence with the mayor or the governor to speed things up?''

''He suggested it.''

''Well?''

''I told him to apply whatever pressure he wanted, but you weren't returning to the shoot until I had some answers.''

''I still think I should have talked to Dom,'' she muttered. ''Explained the situation . . .''

''I explained as much as he needed to know.''

''Right. I can just imagine how warm and friendly that conversation was. I'll be surprised if he's still at the rancho when we get back.''

''I'll be surprised if he isn't.''

As Allie surmised, his conversation with the Zebra had been brief but explosive. Although Rafe had pretty well moved the photographer to the bottom of his list of possible suspects, he still didn't like the man or the way he constantly criticized Allie.

Even now, with her nose shiny and her lips unglossed and her figure encased in a gray sweater reaching almost to her knees, she was perfect in Rafe's mind. Well, almost perfect. Since being confined to this small cabin with her, he'd discovered that Allison Fortune hid a healthy temper of her own behind her porcelain-smooth exterior. Without the outlet of her morning run and the demands of her work, her natural energy spilled over into irritation and this endless pacing.

So much for his intention to see that she got some rest, Rafe thought ruefully.

"I can't believe it," she exclaimed, taking another turn in front of the fireplace. "The flu!"

"Police officers are human. They do get sick once in a while."

Spinning, she planted both hands on her hips. "Don't patronize me. In case you haven't noticed, I'm not in a mood to be rational."

"I've noticed," Rafe drawled.

Allie glared at him, annoyed by his relaxed slouch and too-patient air. She knew darn well what was driving her to this tense, uncharacteristic edginess, and she suspected he did, too. It was one part worry, one part excess energy, and six parts Rafe Stone.

Except for brief excursions to the lodge restaurant for meals, they'd spent their time in this small cabin. Waiting. Maintaining a careful distance from each other. Playing cards with the well-worn deck Rafe discovered among the children's games on the shelves beside the fireplace. Talking, without coming anywhere near the brief intimacy they'd shared last night.

True to his word, Rafe was holding to that damned professional code of his that said he couldn't mix business with personal needs. True to her promise to herself, Allie had refrained from forcing herself on the man. But she was finding it harder and harder to keep that promise with each passing hour.

Getting through the early-morning rituals had been difficult enough. She'd stumbled into the bathroom to find a towel damp from his use. Caught the spicy scent of his after-shave. Seen the tan leather case with his toiletries next to her scarlet-and-gold one. As she stripped and stepped into the shower, Allie couldn't shake the overwhelming awareness that he was only a few steps away.

Allie had spent far longer soaping and shampooing this morning than she usually did. The thought of Rafe in the small cubicle with her, his hard body pressing hers against the old-fashioned tiles, his hands sliding over her slick, sudsy skin, had left her wet and aching... all over.

The long daytime hours that followed had been even worse. The fright from the near accident at the opera had faded in the dazzling sunshine. In any other circumstance, the sharp, clean mountain air would have cleared her mind and her senses. Instead, Rafe's constant presence had taken them close to overload status. Whenever she turned, she'd caught a glimpse of his broad shoulders encased in blue broadcloth. When they went to eat, his touch as he helped her in or out of the car had burned through her layers of sweater and light jacket.

If the early-morning and daylight hours had added to her growing frustration, however, this enforced intimacy of the night made it a hundred times worse. The crackling wood fire threw out a circle of light that drew them within touching distance. The sofa and chairs invited lazy conversation and mindless firewatching. Allie didn't feel the least bit lazy or mindless. She felt itchy and restless and wire-tight.

"You want to try your luck again at gin?" Rafe asked casually.

She gave an unladylike snort. "No way. If we'd been playing for real stakes this afternoon, I'd owe you my net income for the rest of the year. I think you cheated."

"I did," he replied with a crooked grin, locking his hands behind his head.

Allie's stomach lurched. Of all the times for him to turn that rakish lopsided grin on her. They were in the middle of a desperate situation, for heaven's sake. He should be as edgy as she was. At the very least, he could show one or two signs of the racking sensual tension that had kept her tighter than an overwound roll of film all day.

Desperate for something to take her mind off Rafe's nearness, she headed for the built-in shelves beside the fireplace. "Let's see what else we have here. Maybe there's a game you can't deal from the bottom of the deck."

With Allie's back turned to him, Rafe closed his eyes and muttered a fervent prayer that she'd find something, anything, amid the haphazardly stacked boxes to distract her. And him. He wasn't sure how much longer he could maintain this pose of relaxed indifference.

"How about Chinese checkers?" she asked, blowing the dust off a flat box held together with masking tape.

"Fine."

Frowning, she shook the box, then lifted the lid. "Great. No marbles." She replaced the box and pulled out another. "Parcheesi?"

"You'll have to teach me the rules."

"I don't know them."

"We can make them up as we go."

"Sure. And I lose next year's income."

"If you're going to play, you have to pay, Allie."

"So I'm learning," she said under her breath as she shoved the box back in the stack. "So I'm learning."

Frowning, she bent to peer under the lid of another box. Rafe restrained a groan, barely, as her jeans tightened across her thighs and rear. Okay, so long legs constituted a basic requirement for someone in the modeling profession. Did Allie's have to go on for three and a half miles? And end in a perfect, rounded bottom?

She straightened, her face brightening. "Hey, here's a paint-by-number set. I haven't done one of those in years. Want to give it a try?"

Rafe rarely did anything by the numbers, and painting was something he never did at all. If pushing a brush around a piece of cardboard would keep Allie still for a few hours, however, he figured he'd start counting.

"Look," she breathed in delight as she knelt beside the pine-plank coffee table and emptied the box of its contents. "It's a circus scene. A carousel."

Rafe eyed the faint squiggles and numbers dubiously. "How can you tell?"

She didn't appear to hear his question. Her gaze had drifted across the room to the little tin merry-go-round sitting on the nightstand beside the bed.

"I remember how bright and colorful Kate's carousel used to be. All reds and blues and brilliant greens."

Watching her in the firelight, Rafe caught the flicker of pain that crossed her face while she gazed at the little toy. Although he knew the answer, he asked the question anyway.

"Kate?"

"My grandmother," Allie replied softly, her gaze returning to his. "She founded Fortune Cosmetics. She died about six months ago, and . . . I miss her."

He shouldn't do this, Rafe knew. He shouldn't draw Allie out about this grandmother she'd obviously adored. All day long, he'd kept things polite and superficial, determined to reestablish their client-employee relationship. As long as he was responsible for her safety, he wouldn't allow anything else between them.

After this was over, though...

For the first time, Rafe admitted to himself the possibility of an after. He didn't pretend for a moment that this undeniable flash point attraction between them could lead to anything permanent, but while it lasted it could be good. Better than good. Rare and beautiful.

Like Allie.

He'd sworn he wouldn't get involved, wouldn't let another woman complicate his life. Yet, seeing her now in the firelight, he could no more resist trying to ease her pain over her grandmother's death than he could stop breathing.

Rafe didn't fight the fierce tide of protectiveness that slammed through him. What had begun as a job was now an elemental need. He wanted to shield Allie from every hurt, including the sadness that darkened her eyes to a deep, fathomless brown.

"What was she like?" he asked quietly, sensing that this woman who kept so much of herself hidden behind her smiling public facade needed to talk, to share some of her loss. Rafe suspected her twin normally served as Allie's outlet. Tonight, she had only him.

"Kate was a lot like you," she answered after a moment. "Gutsy and tough and independent as the dickens. She was piloting her own plane over the Amazon when it went down."

"She sounds like quite a woman."

The carousel drew her gaze once more. "She was."

Curling his hands into fists to keep from dragging her into his arms, Rafe searched for a nonphysical way to comfort her.

"Why don't we use those paints to restore your grandmother's carousel?" he suggested. "While we work, you can tell me more about her."

Allie swung her head around, surprise chasing the shadows from her eyes. "What a wonderful idea! Do you know how to paint?"

"What's to know? You just slap a brush into one of those plastic jobbies of paint and splash some color on."

"Hmm..." She cocked her head. "Why do I think this little exercise is going to be more of a challenge than playing gin?"

Sharing the small table beside the window and a half-dozen plastic containers of oil paint with Rafe was more than a challenge, Allie discovered some time later. It was a threat to her restraint.

More than once, her heart thumped at the sight of his dark head bent as he hunched over the little toy, his big hand wielding a paintbrush no thicker than an average-size toothpick. Allie spent as much time watching his progress as making any of her own. Whenever a hard thigh accidentally bumped hers under the small table or an elbow nudged hers, she didn't make any progress at all.

As the hours slid by, she found herself telling Rafe about the entire Fortune clan. About fiery, feisty Kate.

About her parents' growing estrangement. About the joys and drawbacks of being a twin in a large, boisterous family.

"Rocky and I loved switching identities when we were young," she confided, squinting as she drew a fine line of red along the halter of a tiny prancing horse. "Occasionally it backfired, though. Like the time she went out with one of my boyfriends and he ended up falling for her, big-time."

Rafe scrunched his forehead and daubed a blob of green on an upturned muzzle. "The guy must have been a real jerk," he commented absently. "Right up there in the Viking category. I can't imagine a boyfriend not being able to tell you two apart."

She twirled the tip of her brush in the plastic paint container. "Can't you? That's because you saw Rocky in her leather flight jacket and jeans. When she's not wearing her Red Baron gear, she's...she's..."

She was Rocky. There was no other way to describe her.

"She's not you, Allie," he muttered, concentrating on his artwork. "Whatever or whoever she is, she's not you."

Startled by his uncanny echo of her thoughts, Allie's hand stilled.

"I'd say the two of you are like this little toy your grandmother left you," Rafe mused, dipping his green-tipped brush into the container of orange and starting in on the mane. "The outer shell doesn't matter. It's the song within that makes you what you are.''

Allie stared at his bent head, her throat tight. In a few succinct phrases, he'd articulated the haunting beauty of her inheritance. Yet she sensed that he still didn't see its applicability to himself. Or, if he did, he wasn't ready to admit it.

He gave a little grunt and laid his brush down. "Not bad, if I do say so myself.''

She glanced from the gaudily painted horse to see the smug satisfaction on his face and felt her heart thump once, very painfully. Then he grinned at her, and that same organ went into total meltdown.

In that instant, Allie had the horrible suspicion that she loved him. She'd known that what she felt for this man went beyond mere lust. She'd entertained the secret hope that the attraction sizzling between them might develop into something more after the shoot. Until this moment, though, she'd defined that something as a loose, vague relationship...a testing and trying and exploring.

She wasn't ready for love, she thought in sudden panic. Not yet. She'd almost made one disastrous mistake with a fiancé she thought she knew and didn't. She couldn't be in love with a man she hardly knew at all.

Especially not with this one. He irritated her as much as he intrigued her. He had an annoying habit of standing back and letting her fend off other men's advances, and stubbornly refusing to advance himself. So far, she'd made every move in this cautious, tumultuous mating dance of theirs.

Yet she felt safe with him, Allie acknowledged. And wildly free when they ran together. And totally, erotically female when he took her in his arms.

Shaken, she put down her paintbrush. She had to think about this. Seriously. Pushing her chair back, she rose and dusted her hands on the back of her sweater.

"It's late. I, uh... Maybe we should finish this tomorrow? Do you want the bathroom first?"

"You go ahead. I'll finish this mane, then clean the brushes."

Allie left him bent over the toy, a strand of dark hair spilling over his forehead as he hunched down to stroke the brush along a flowing mane. Snatching her sleepshirt off the bed, she closed herself in the bathroom. She stripped, then grimaced when she realized that she'd been too shaken to gather clean underwear.

She stepped out of the bathroom some time later, wearing only her nightshirt. At that moment, Rafe shoved back his chair and rose. His back to Allie, he stretched.

She stopped abruptly, mesmerized by the pantherlike grace and utter masculinity of the lazy movement. His blue shirt shaped a form at once lean and powerful. The artist in her focused on the perfect balance between line and form. The woman in her tightened in response.

Suddenly, he froze in midstretch, his whole body tensing. Wincing, he lifted his bent arm and slowly brought his elbow forward.

Guilt stabbed through Allie like a sharp, serrated knife. Only last night, he'd admitted to her that the grafted skin pulled at times. Obviously, this was one of those times. Yet he'd hunched over her merry-go-round for hours in an attempt to keep her occupied.

Turning on her heel, she marched back into the bathroom and dug through her cosmetic kit. When she emerged again a few moments later, she had a thick plastic tube in one hand.

"Done?" Rafe asked, raking her bare legs with a quick glance.

"No. Not quite. I've got one more task to do tonight." She glanced around the room, then aimed the tube at the sturdy pine-plank coffee table.

"Sit."

"What?"

"Sit down. Over there, by the fire."

"Why?" he asked, eyeing the tube with some suspicion.

"I saw you wince and try to stretch your shoulder a little while ago. I told you last night, I've got something that could help. We're going to try a little massage."

"It's okay. You don't need to—"

"Yes, I do."

"Look, it's fine. I don't—"

"Sit!"

Rafe lifted a black brow. For long moments, he studied the determined expression on her face.

"Do you have any idea how much you look and sound like your father right now? He doesn't know how to take no for an answer, either."

Folding her arms, Allie tapped a bare foot.

"All right, all right."

Reluctance was etched in every line of his body as he moved toward the fireplace. His fingers worked the buttons on his blue shirt, and then he tugged out the shirttails and slipped it off. Allie held her breath as he reached for the hem of his white T-shirt. Slowly he drew it over his head and tossed it on the sofa.

She could do this, she told herself. She could squeeze a dab of cream onto her hands, warm it between her palms, and smooth it over his shoulder without dissolving into a puddle of liquid need at the touch of her hands on him. She could stand behind him, her bare knees pressing gently against his buttocks while she worked the lotion into his skin, and not bend to kiss the hard ridges.

Maybe.

Her hands kneaded his shoulder. Massaged his back. His flesh felt warm under her fingertips, his muscles tight.

"Try to relax, Rafe."

He didn't reply.

Her thumbs moved in a counterrhythm to her fingers. Sweep, and gently squeeze. Smooth, and dig firmly into the resisting tissue. The dying fire flickered and wrapped them in an intimate circle of golden light. As the silent moments passed, Allie felt a primitive, instinctive awareness seep into her.

She suspected this was how things had always been. A man reluctant to admit weakness. A woman having to assert her own strength to care for him.

The incipient panic that had attacked her earlier disappeared in the absolute rightness of the moment. She wanted to care for this man, always. She ached to match her differing strength to his and join their separate halves into a stronger whole.

Grimly Allie recalled her pledge not to force herself on him again. He had to come to her. He had to take the next step.

Feel me, she urged silently. *Feel the touch of my hands on you and the need in my heart.*

His skin was warmer now, but every bit as tense. She splayed her hands across the small of his back and worked upward.

Feel my fire. My heat.

Her fingers ached by the time she angled to his side and began to work the cream into his shoulder and the underside of his chin. His arm shifted, brushing against her breasts.

Touch me, Rafe. Touch me as I'm touching you.

She shaped the strong column of his throat. Stroking. Creaming. Loving.

He stared straight into the fire, his jaw as rigid as his body. Allie fought the urge to kiss the fine lines at the corners of his eyes. To taste the faint sheen that dampened his brow.

Heat coursed through his skin now, burning her wherever she made contact. Her breasts ached, their tips hard and tight. Her stomach clenched.

He shifted again, brushing against her. Her womb tightened.

Now, Rafe. Please.

"Allie?" His voice was low, harsh,

Her hands stilled. "What?"

"Are you wearing anything under that shirt?"

She wet her lips. "No."

"That's what I was afraid of."

For long moments, neither of them moved. Then Rafe slowly slewed around and captured her between his knees. His hands rested on her hips, hers on his shoulders.

Allie stood before him. Waiting. Hoping. Afraid to take more than a shallow breath. When he raised his eyes to hers again, they held a combination of reluctant surrender and blue fire that made her heart leap.

"One good massage deserves another, sweetheart. Where's that tube of grease?"

Her hand shaking, she passed him one of the products Fortune Cosmetics had banked its entire future on.

This time their loving was slow and deliberate and incredibly erotic.

Rafe kept her caged between his thighs, naked and trembling. As he rubbed his palms together to warm the cream, he feasted his eyes on her breasts and belly and the dark red triangle between her legs. Where it wasn't kissed by shadows, her skin glowed golden in the flickering firelight.

He wasn't quite sure exactly when or how he'd decided to abandon his rigid determination to keep his hands off Allie and his mind on his job. During the past few minutes, her need had somehow fired his own, well past the point of resistance. What he wanted from, and for, this red-and-gold, dusky-tipped woman now had no anchor in reality. Reality was yesterday, and tomorrow. Tonight was Allie's alone.

At the touch of his hands, her belly jerked and her breasts quivered. He gentled her as he would a nervous bird, with low words and soft strokes.

"Easy, sweetheart. Easy."

He spread the cream onto her hips. His fingers kneaded the slender curves while his thumbs rotated on the flat surface of her stomach. A slight pressure brought her closer. His hands slid down the slope of her rear, massaging her and stroking and lifting her onto her toes in a shiver of excitement.

Slowly he brought his hands up her back, rubbing gently at the knots of tension in her spine. His palms eased around her rib cage and lifted the soft weights of her breasts. Rafe took the tip of one in his mouth, tasting her sweetness while he suckled.

"Oh!"

She arched back, bowing. His thighs parted slightly. Holding her still with one hand, he slid his other down her belly.

"Open for me, Allie," he murmured against her breast.

The inside of her thighs clenched, then loosened. Rafe felt the spasmodic movement as he speared his fingers through the silky curls at the apex of her legs. He pressed lower, parting her folds, and continued his erotic massage, his thumb rotating against her sensitive flesh.

Tremors shook her. Dampness dewed his hand. Rafe used his teeth on the tight bud of her breast, nipping it into a thrusting point. Her head fell back as he brought the other to matching stiffness.

He leaned away from her, his heart tripping as he took in her wild beauty. It held no trace of the sophisticated, glamorous supermodel. No sign of the laughing jogger who could still run circles around him in the cool dawn, or of the black-gowned opera aficionado whose elegance came from within.

This was a pagan goddess. A creature of flame and liquid heat. A woman unashamed of her own sensuality and the pleasure he brought her. She gloried in her passion, and it took every ounce of strength Rafe possessed to curb his own until he satisfied hers.

When he eased his hand from its wet, silken nest, she groaned a protest. Smiling, Rafe bent to replace his hand with his mouth. She arched backward, her small cry echoing through the cabin. He drank his fill of her, or tried to. While his senses registered honey and musk, his mind accepted the fact that he'd never get enough of Allie.

A series of uncontrolled tremors told him she was nearing her peak. Keeping her legs spread and her desire primed, he shed his few remaining clothes. Taking time only to protect her from a pregnancy neither of them was ready for, he brought her down into his lap.

Allie gasped when he slid into her. Then she wrapped her legs around his waist and her arms around his neck and covered his mouth with hers. As her climax neared, she moaned and buried her face in his neck.

"Oh, Rafe," she murmured in a ragged, throaty whisper. "I seriously think I could love you."

Limp with pleasure, Allie clung to Rafe's neck when he carried her across the room some time later. She made no effort to convince him to join her under the down comforter. She didn't have to. He pulled back the covers and eased into them with her still cradled in his arms. She stretched out beside him, her body pressed to his. With unerring instinct, her nose found the warm crease between his shoulder and neck.

She felt exalted and exhilarated and too exhausted for words. Sleep tugged at her, overriding the tiny worry that squiggled around at the back of her mind. She shouldn't have whispered that she could love him. Desperately. Her feelings were too new. Too uncertain for her to press them on him yet. Yet the words had slipped out during the peak of her passion, and she couldn't recall them. Or regret them.

That was a worry for yesterday, she decided. Or tomorrow. Right now, she would focus only on his warmth next to her in the bed, his breath on her shoulder, and his arms around her.

Twelve

Allie woke the next morning to a narrow beam of sunlight slicing through the edges of the drawn curtains and an empty cabin.

Pushing her tangled hair out of her eyes, she rose up on one elbow. A quick survey convinced her that Rafe had left while she was still sleeping. Sudden doubt rushed through her, only to be shoved aside with the covers. Whatever else he might decide to do after last night, Rafe wouldn't leave her unprotected.

Her bet was that he'd gone to the restaurant to procure the caffeine he needed to jumpstart his system. And breakfast, she guessed. The Devil's Peak version of *chila*-whatevers. He'd tried to get her to try the mysterious dish yesterday, but she'd been too edgy and tense over the incident at the opera and the delay in the schedule to abandon her diet, as well. This morning, she could eat a moose slathered in green chilis. Or Rafe slathered in anything, she decided, grinning.

She was dressed and waiting when he returned some fifteen minutes later. Sure enough, he carried a plastic tray loaded with two large foam cups and several boxes of assorted sizes. She answered his knock and stepped back as he brought a gust of pine-scented mountain air with him into the cabin. He stopped just over the threshold and let his gaze roam from the top of her brushed and shining hair to the white athletic socks she'd appropriated from his carryall.

He hadn't showered or shaved, Allie saw, no doubt to keep from waking her. Stubble darkened his chin and his lower cheeks, and his hair was ruffled from the breeze outside. He looked dark and rugged and altogether too serious for the morning after one of the most glorious nights of her life.

Drawing in a deep breath, Allie willed him to kiss her. She balled her fists behind her back and focused all her energy on sending him a mental message.

Touch me, Rafe. Kiss me.

To her delight, he set the tray down on the table against the wall and curled a knuckle under her chin. His hand was still cool from the chill morning air, yet Allie burned where he touched her.

She saw a raw hunger in his eyes that more than matched her own, and a worry that told her he'd brought back more than just breakfast. Determinedly ignoring the worry for the moment, she closed her eyes and reveled in his kiss. When she opened them again, her mouth curved in a small smile.

"Nice," she murmured.

"Very."

"And definitely undumb."

"One of the undumbest things I've ever done," he agreed, brushing his thumb across her lower lip. Then he stepped back to shrug out of his sheepskin vest, and Allie knew she couldn't ignore the worry any longer.

"Did you talk to the police?"

Nodding, he hung his vest on the back of one of the chairs. "I called them from the restaurant."

"And?"

His jaw tightened. "And they've drawn a blank. On both fronts. There's no record of any call being made to your room from the mobile phone in the processing center."

Allie sagged in relief. "I knew no one on the crew could be harassing me like that."

"This doesn't rule them out," Rafe countered sharply. "It just means that the call wasn't made from the processing unit. Someone could have made it easily from outside the rancho."

"Okay, okay! What about the incident at the opera?"

He shook his head. "The rubber coating on the cable is too porous. The lab could lift only a few smudges."

Allie's initial relief gave way to crushing disappointment. She'd hoped desperately that the police would identify some stranger, some fanatic, who'd followed her to Santa Fe and mingled with the crowd at the gala. She wanted this harassment to end.

"There's more," he continued, his mouth grim. "The lab can't state with any degree of certainty whether the cable was cut deliberately or simply worn through by the same kind of sharp edge that sliced into my tux.''

"So it might have been an accident after all?''

"It might.''

"The caller might not even be here? In Santa Fe?''

"He could be anywhere.'' Frustration evident in every line of his taut body, Rafe raked a hand through his hair. "It looks like we're back to square one.''

Allie shoved aside her bitter disappointment. "Oh, no,'' she replied softly. "Not square one. I'm not sure exactly where we are, but not square one.''

He glanced at her, his tension taking on a hint of wary confusion. Allie had experienced the same confusion last night, only hers had come closer to panic.

"I'm not exactly sure where we are, either,'' he said slowly. "All I know is that I've broken just about every rule in my book since I met you, lady.''

"Yes, well, rules are made to be broken, or at least modified to fit the circumstances.''

Although Allie kept her tone light, she suspected her smile came out a bit lopsided. Dammit! She shouldn't have scared him with that silly whispered promise of almost-love. She'd spooked him, as his next words proved.

"I was married once, Allie.''

"I know.''

"It didn't work.''

"So? I was almost married once. That didn't work, either.''

"You don't understand. I wasn't particularly choice husband material before the explosion. My wife decided I was even less of a catch afterward. Now..."

"Now, you're a little dented and scarred, like the carousel," Allie interrupted, mentally consigning the ex-Mrs. Stone to a pit of hungry vipers. *Very* hungry vipers.

"More than a little, sweetheart."

"You said yourself that it didn't matter what the outside shell looked like. It's the song inside that counts. I, for one, happen to like the way you sing," she finished fiercely.

One corner of his mouth curled. "You do, huh?"

"I do. Well, most of the time," she amended. "When you're not going on about zebras and cigars and such."

"Guess I'll have to watch what I say about your collection. While I wasn't looking, I seem to have become part of it."

She'd have to think about that one, Allie decided, tucking it away for future examination.

"Don't look so worried," she told him. "I won't push you into anything you're not ready for."

A rueful gleam lightened his eyes to a silvery blue. "You've been pushing me since the moment I laid eyes on you, Miss Fortune."

"Is that so?"

He brushed a knuckle down her cheek. "You know damn well that's so."

She bit back the retort that certain men needed to be pushed, either into the lake or into love. Curling a hand over his, she nuzzled her cheek against his palm.

"I'm serious, Rafe. We'll play this by... by whatever rules you want to establish. Within reason, of course."

"Why do I sense that I might have come up with a whole new set of rules?"

Allie hid her relief. He hadn't exactly committed to anything like a future together, but neither had he turned tail and run. After all the years she'd spent holding off men who proclaimed to be in love with her, or at least her face, she was finding this business of coaxing Rafe into her bed and her heart a bit daunting. Deciding she'd pushed him enough, she dropped her hand and pulled out a chair.

"I'll help you write them," she promised. "Right now, though, I guess we'd better eat and get packed. If we make it back to Rancho Tremayo by noon, we might be able to get the museum sequence done this afternoon."

"I'm not sure we should go back to Rancho Tremayo. Not yet."

She paused in the act of prying a lid off one of the cartons. "Why not?"

Rafe hooked a chair and sat down opposite her. "I can't give you a specific reason, just a gut feeling. Although I don't have any proof, my instinct tells me the calls are from someone you know. Someone who knows your schedule. I want to run some more background checks."

"I thought you already ran checks on everyone, me included?"

"I did."

Frowning, Allie watched as Rafe dug a fork into a congealing mass of eggs, vegetables, diced ham and green chilis. She shuddered, remembering her earlier confidence that she could eat a moose slathered with that stuff. Thank goodness Rafe had brought her wheat toast and fruit instead.

"There has to be something I'm missing," he said between forkfuls. "I'll just have to dig deeper."

Allie crumbled a sliver of dry toast in her fingers, torn. She understood his determination. He was a professional—one of the best in the business, according to her father. So was she.

"How long will this excavation take?"

"As long as necessary. Until I come up with something that feels right," he said grimly.

Torn, Allie tried to weigh his gut instinct against the weight of her responsibility to her family and to the rest of the crew. As much as she longed to spend another few days with Rafe in this isolated mountain cabin, she couldn't keep a crew of forty hanging around, twiddling their thumbs, without good cause. And she was too much a Fortune to let the company Kate had built with her own hands founder in the process.

"Rafe, I have to go back. We've already lost a day and a half in the schedule."

His black brows slanted. "Didn't I just hear you agree to play this by my rules . . . again?"

"I did . . . within reason." She hesitated, groping for the right words. "I'm not particularly brave or adventuresome, like Kate was. It scares me to think someone I know may be trying to harm me, or to harm my family through me."

"I don't care much for the idea, either."

"Yet if I let him frighten me into canceling the shoot and delaying the launch of this new product line, he's done just that."

"Allie . . ."

She reached across the table and gripped his hand. "There's more at stake here than most people realize, Rafe. My grandmother's company in on the line. My family's future. I can't let them—or her memory—down."

He stared at her for long moments, his face hard-set and unyielding. Then his breath slowly gusted out.

"From what you told me about your grandmother last night, I'd say you've got more of her gritty courage than you realize."

Allie managed a lopsided smile. "I've also got you guarding my person."

"Yeah, well, that's one of the rules we're going to revise immediately. From here on out, Miss Fortune, I'm not guarding your person from the next casita."

Soft laughter spilled through her. "Now that, Mr. Stone, is one rule I can live with."

They arrived back at Rancho Tremayo just before noon. As Allie had predicted, the delay in the production schedule had turned Dom from surly and sarcastic to savage. The photographer's mood wasn't improved by a further delay while his assistant scurried to round up the rest of the crew. Or by Rafe's quiet announcement that he was moving his gear into Allie's casita immediately following the afternoon's shoot.

The bald half of the Zebra's head went red, along with the whole of his face. He glared at Rafe with undisguised dislike, his lip curling back in a sneer.

"Apparently Allie got more recreation than rest during her little R and R."

"Watch it, Avendez."

Rafe's soft warning deepened the red stain, but the photographer didn't back down.

"I've known Allie a lot longer than you have, Stone. I've watched men fall all over her, dazzled by the woman they think she is. Very few ever get past her outer shell, or see what I see through the viewfinder."

A collage of images instantly filled Rafe's mind. Of Allie's laughing face as she sprawled atop him in the dust.

Of a scrubbed and nightshirt-clad woman standing in the middle of the cabin, pointing a tube of skin cream at the coffee table and sternly ordering him to sit.

Of a glorious pagan goddess, her head thrown back, her skin tinted to gold by the fire.

At that moment, Rafe knew he'd been given a rare and precious gift. He'd viewed something Avendez would never see through his camera lens. The knowledge softened his instinctive antagonism toward the photographer.

"Maybe you do see something through the viewfinder that few others are privileged to see," he said quietly. "You and Allie know how to use your skills to bring out the best in each other. But I'm moving my things into her casita after the shoot."

For a moment longer, Avendez held his eyes, still angry, still rawly jealous. Then the flush staining his face slowly faded, and his shoulders sagged.

"Fine. But until then, she's mine."

Rafe didn't argue. He knew as well as Avendez that Allie belonged to no one but herself. What she chose to give to others was a gift.

By the time the hastily assembled team had gathered in the courtyard, the photographer had recovered his acidic tongue. He lashed out at everyone indiscriminately as they hastily loaded the equipment into vehicles and headed into Santa Fe. Following the small convoy, Rafe drove Allie to the internationally renowned Museum of Indian Arts and Culture, a soaring structure of adobe and glass that housed one of the world's foremost collections of Native American artifacts.

While Xola combed the museum for usable props, Avendez positioned his model against a backdrop of priceless Anasazi pottery to capture what he called her timeless essence. Throughout the process, Rafe's eyes roamed the scene.

A splotch of burnt orange snared his attention. His eyes thoughtful, he watched the sweatshirt-clad Geek jump every time Avendez shouted at him to move the reflector or get a goddamn fan and make a breeze to ruffle Allie's skirt. Granted, working around the Zebra would make anyone a prime candidate for a psych ward. But the kid's jerky nervousness seemed to peak two thirds of the way through the shoot, when he dropped a whole tray of exposed film and roused Dom to unprecedented fury.

Scrambling awkwardly on hands and knees to retrieve the film, Philips stuffed it into the tray and scurried for a supply of fresh film. He returned some time later, swiping his arm across his nose like a kid who'd had a good cry.

Suddenly Rafe stiffened.

A doper! he thought, totally disgusted with himself for not picking up on it sooner. The kid was a doper! A sometime user, or the signs would have been more visible. Still, Rafe shouldn't have missed the runny nose, a classic symptom of a snorter.

Eyes narrowed, he watched Philips skulk at the back of the shoot. A thousand possibilities sifted through his mind. Drugs could have magnified an otherwise healthy young male's fascination with Allie Fortune's beautiful image into a sick fixation. The kid could have made the calls when he was high, so high he either didn't remember them or managed to disguise all evidence of his obsession when he was down. He could have...

"Dammit, I want this shot backlit, not silhouetted. You can't even see her face. Move that damn strobe."

While Avendez snarled in fury at his hapless team, Rafe watched the Geek closely. He'd visit the kid later tonight, he decided with grim determination. It was time they had another little chat.

The exhausted crew returned to Rancho Tremayo some seven hours later. Leaving Allie in her casita for a few moments, Rafe went next door to collect his gear. When he returned, she had showered and changed.

"Dom wants to go over the contact sheets in the processing unit," she told him with a tired smile. "His team will print whatever shots we decide to go with from today's sequence while we review tomorrow's production schedule."

"Give me five minutes," Rafe replied, dumping his gear on the bed.

As he walked through the cool, starry night to his casita, Rafe realized he'd have to delay his private conversation with the Geek. Although his instincts told him to corner the kid now, before anything else happened, Allie was totally depleted from the grueling seven-hour shoot. On top of that, she had this late-night conference to get through. She needed sleep, badly, and Rafe wasn't about to leave her alone in her casita or her bed.

He'd pull the kid aside tomorrow, he decided. After the morning run, while Allie was safely ensconced with her team of stylists and makeup artists and hairdressers. Right now, though, he'd make a quick call to New York and get the detective working Allie's case to check the National Crime Information Center for priors on one Jerome Philips. If the Geek had any history of arrests for drug use, it would show up in NCIC's computers.

As the intense review session dragged on, Allie was too exhausted to take more than passing notice of Rafe's coiled tension. Her eyes blurring, she propped her chin in her elbows and surveyed the black-and-white contact sheets on the worktable.

"This one, I think," Dom muttered. The felt tip of his marker squeaked as he circled a shot of Allie running a finger around the lip of a breathtakingly beautiful black pottery bowl.

She scrunched her nose. Combined with the scent of developing solution and the other chemicals stored in the unit, the odor from the marker was giving her a headache. Allie wanted desperately to be out of the closed-in unit, walking through the clean air with Rafe. Or snuggled up beside him in the wide bed in her casita. Or sprawled on top of him in...

"What do you think, Allie?"

She blinked and focused her tired eyes on the contact sheet. "Of which one?"

Dom's mouth screwed into a tight line. "This one," he said acidly, tapping his marker against the sheet. "The one that just might win me an Addie this year, not to mention sell every tube of Sunglazed Wine that Fortune Cosmetics can produce."

Startled, Allie peered at the shot in question. It was a head-and-shoulders, with her face turned slightly to the left. Her chin tipped upward. Her lustrous dark red lips were parted in a small half smile. Dom had flash-fired through a softbox to slightly blur the wall behind her, which was patterned with ancient Anasazi symbols. Enough of the texture remained, however, to hint at the mysterious past.

It was a striking portrait of now and then. Of a living, breathing woman and a long-dead civilization. Of the continuum of time. It also, Allie noted with an experienced eye, drew the viewer's glance to a mouth glossed with Fortune Cosmetics's newest fall shade.

At that moment, she fully shared Dom's confidence that the shot could win him the prestigious Addie award from the National Council on Advertising. Hopefully it would also entice a whole continent of women to try Sunglazed Wine and its sister colors.

"It's good, Dom," she said quietly. "Very good. I think we should use it for the two-page color spread we bought in *Cosmo.*"

"I think so, too."

The others crowded around the table to examine the shot. Dom's senior assistants, Xola and the art director all offered their comments. The discussion rose in waves, hot and heavy. Then Dom thrust the contact sheet at the intern and sent him into the darkroom at the back of the unit to make prints of the circled shots.

Grabbing the next sheet, Dom hunched over the table. Wearily Allie slumped in her chair. Her eyes met Rafe's over the others' heads. He looked as tired as she felt, she thought. The tension of the past few days, not to mention their rather strenuous activity last night, had etched a web of fine lines at the corners of his eyes. Deep grooves bracketed his mouth, a mouth Allie longed to kiss. Above the open collar of his blue cotton shirt, his chin wore a late-night shadow. Although he sat on a tall stool with lazy grace, one boot propped on the rung, she could see the tight lines in his shoulders.

Scooting her chair back, she rolled her neck to ease the ache and moved to Rafe's side.

"Tired?" she asked softly over the buzz of heated conversation from the table.

He shrugged. "A little. Not as much as you are, I suspect. Here, turn around."

Shifting her within the V of his knees, he began to massage her neck and shoulders. His kneading fingers worked magic on Allie's tight muscles.

Slowly she sloughed off her weariness like a discarded skin. This was good, she thought with a leisurely spiral of delight. Very good. She didn't even have to will him to touch her.

By the time she turned back to face him, her eyes were alight with promise. "That was wonderful. I'll return the favor when we get back to the casita. I've still got a good supply of that miracle cream left."

Rafe's mouth curved in a crooked grin. "I don't think I'll need any miracles tonight."

"I wouldn't be so sure, tough guy. Remember, I'm a professional model. I can hold a position for hours."

The buzz of the portable phone cut off Rafe's rumble of laughter. Dom snatched the receiver out of the leather box, clearly displeased with the interruption.

"What?" he barked. "Yeah, okay."

Slamming the receiver down, he shot Rafe an unfriendly glare. "There's a fax coming in for you at the front desk. From New York. The desk clerk says it's stamped Immediate Attention."

The tension Rafe had pushed aside during these stolen moments with Allie clamped on to his neck with the force of a vise. His gut tightened as she slewed around, her eyes wide.

"New York?"

He nodded. "I made a call earlier. This might be in answer to it."

"You'd better go get it."

Rafe hesitated, not wanting to leave her alone, even for the few moments it would take to cross the courtyard to the main building. Frowning, he glanced at the group crowded around the table.

"How much longer are you going to be here?" he asked Avendez.

"If you'd stop pawing Allie and let her get back to work, we could be done in a half hour or less."

"Go get it, Rafe," Allie urged quietly. "I'll be all right here."

"Do you have your beeper?"

She patted her pant leg, nodding.

"I'll be right back."

Rafe strode across the courtyard, his boot heels clicking on the tiles. Brushing past the sleepy-eyed doorman, he headed for the front desk. The clerk smiled a greeting, then lifted her shoulders apologetically when he asked for his fax.

"I'm sorry, Mr. Stone. The machine jammed on the cover page. I called the sender and asked them to retransmit. It should be here in just a few minutes."

Rafe bit back both a curse and the urge to inform the clerk that Rancho Tremayo's fax system was about as efficient as its voice mail. He snagged a cup of coffee from the pot kept ready for late-night guests, blowing at the steam while he cooled his heels in the foyer. His impatience mounted with each passing minute, as did his uneasiness. The detective must have discovered something very interesting from NCIC to be sending it over the wires this late.

He checked his watch, noting that it was well after 2:00 a.m. in New York. And a good fifteen minutes since the clerk had called.

"How about checking on that fax?"

She glanced up, all placating smiles. "I haven't heard the machine in the back room beep."

"Check it," he growled.

Her smile slipped. "Yes, sir."

As it turned out, Rafe never got to see the fax. He was still waiting impatiently at the counter when the beeper in his pocket sounded a steady alarm.

Thirteen

Ever afterward, Allie would remember the sequence of events that night in a stark, slow-moving dreamscape, like an old movie played over and over at the wrong speed. Everything happened so fast, and yet seemed to last ten lifetimes.

One moment, she was rubbing her temple to ease the strain of the incipient headache caused by the smell of developing fluid and Magic Marker.

The next, Dom was gathering up the contact sheets and stuffing them in a folder. Tossing the folder into a drawer, he stood. The others looked up at him in surprise.

"Aren't we going to go over tomorrow's production schedule?" the art director asked in surprise.

"Not tonight," he said brusquely. "We're all too tired to see straight. We'll go over it in the morning. Come on, let's walk our star back to her casita and see if we can locate her watchdog on the way."

Allie rose and stretched, a sensual lassitude sliding through her at the thought of locating Rafe and locking herself into her casita with him. She'd have him beside her all through the night. If they wound up this shoot tomorrow, and that fax from New York resolved the mystery of her calls, then maybe she'd have him through all the nights to come. Away from Dom, away from the crew and the stress of the past weeks, they'd have time to explore each other. To rewrite the rest of his precious rules.

Her weariness tripping into anticipation, Allie followed Dom and the others to the door. She reached for the switch as she went out, intending to turn off the lights.

"Leave them," Dom instructed. "I'm coming back."

"I thought you said we were all too tired to see straight."

"Yeah, well, some of us are. Come on, kid. Let's get you tucked in." He started to hook an arm around her neck, then caught himself. "Guess I'll have to remember not to do that. Your *friend* doesn't seem to like it."

Allie heard the challenge behind his sneer, and the need for reassurance. Snagging his arm, she pulled him back a few paces. Xola turned and eyed them curiously, her face an unreadable mask in the dim light cast by the lanterns in the courtyard.

"Rafe thinks it's impossible for a man to be friends with a woman he lusts for," Allie said quietly. "I . . . I'm beginning to think the same holds true for a woman."

The photographer grimaced. "You don't have to tell me you lust after him. I'm the one on the other side of the viewfinder, remember? I've seen every panting little look you've sneaked his way."

Allie smiled and tugged on a lock of his flowing black hair. "It's gone beyond lust, Dom. At least on my side. I think... I'm pretty sure I'm in love with him."

He didn't reply for several seconds. Allie thought she caught a flicker of pain, quickly hidden, but she knew there was nothing she could do about it except be honest with him... and be his friend.

"You've thought you were in love before, Allie. You were all set to have me shoot a wedding portrait, as I recall."

"I know." She fell back on the age-old explanation for all things that can't be explained. "This is different."

"You sure?"

"I'm sure."

Dom's shoulders drooped infinitesimally, then lifted in a shrug. "Hell. I suppose I'll have to do another portrait of you for a groom's present."

She grinned at his thoroughly disgusted expression. "I hope so."

He hesitated, then answered her grin with a smile. "I can't think of any portrait more perfect than the one we picked tonight for the *Cosmo* ad."

"Oh, Dom," Allie breathed. "That shot would be perfect! Something from New Mexico. From our time together here."

"God, don't go all squeaky and gushy and super-modelly on me," he said gruffly. "Let me go get the contact sheet. You can show it to this jerk you're pretty sure you're in love with and tell me if that's the one he wants."

She started to nod, then caught sight of Xola. For an unguarded moment, naked longing showed on the other woman's face. Allie caught Dom's arm as he turned to head back toward the processing unit.

"Wait. I'll get it. You'd better explain to Xola what I'm doing, though. I don't want her thinking I'm messing with any of the props she's pulled together for tomorrow."

Giving Dom a gentle shove in the stylist's direction, Allie walked back to the unit. She stepped inside and let the door bang behind her as she walked to the desk. Pulling out the folder she'd seen Dom stuff the contact sheets in, she shuffled through them. When she didn't find the one she wanted, she fanned through the sheets again.

It took her a moment to remember that Dom had given it to Jerry to take to the darkroom at the back of the processing center to develop. She was halfway to the darkroom when she noticed a faint glow of light under its door. Frowning, she stared at the strip of gold, then stopped suddenly.

She remembered Jerry heading for the darkroom, but she couldn't remember whether he'd come out or left with the crowd of others. Recalling Rafe's suspicions about the intern, Allie started to back up. At that moment, the door opened and Jerry stepped out, swiping the back of his hand across his nose.

He jerked to a stop when he saw Allie, his eyes widening. Then he frowned and scanned the empty room behind her.

"Where is everyone?"

"We decided to quit early," she replied. "They're waiting outside."

His nostrils flared, and he sucked in a quick breath as he stared at Allie. "Why are you here?"

The sudden intensity of his gaze unnerved Allie. She edged backward.

"I, uh, came back for one of contact sheets. Look, I didn't know you were here. I mean, I forgot you were working in the darkroom. I didn't mean to disturb you."

Allie knew she was babbling, but Jerry's stare had raised the hairs on the back of her neck. Her hand crept into her pocket. She took another step back, and felt her legs bump against the table.

"I'll just get the sheet tomorrow," she told him. "When you're not busy."

"Wait."

At his growled command, her startled gaze flew back to his face. His voice had dropped, almost to a whisper.

"No, really. I'm tired. I'll . . ."

Jerry's gaze slid to the shelves of supplies beside him. While Allie edged around the table toward the door, his hand darted out and closed around a glass bottle filled with orange liquid.

It was only indicator stop bath, she told herself, trying not to panic. He needed it to process the prints. Despite her best efforts to keep calm, her hand shook as she reached for the door and started to pull it open.

He was beside her instantly, his palm slamming against the door. Allie jumped back. She squeezed the beeper in her pocket at the same instant he lifted the jar and twisted off its cap.

A corrosive chemical odor tainted the air, adding to the coppery tang of fear swamping Allie's senses. She opened her mouth to call out, then snapped it shut when he lifted the jar menacingly.

"Don't scream, Allison," he ordered softly.

Allison! He called her *Allison!*

Rafe was right, she thought, her throat clogging with fear. He was right.

"Don't call out to the others. I don't want to hurt you more than I have to."

Oh, God! She squeezed her fist around the beeper as hard as she could. *Rafe! Please, Rafe! Hurry!*

Wiping her tongue across her lips, she backed away as far as the close confines of the unit would allow. One thigh hit the stool Rafe had perched on earlier. Allie groped behind her with her free hand, never releasing her death grip on the beeper.

"Why are you doing this?"

"I have to."

"Why, Jerry? I...I thought we were friends. I thought you...you liked working with me."

"I do. I'm sorry, Allison."

Keeping his eyes locked on her face, he fumbled with the bolt to the door. Allie tried frantically to distract him while she scrabbled for a grip on the stool. If she could get a good enough hold to swing it one-handed, she might deflect enough of the corrosive chemical to keep it out of her eyes.

"Why, Jerry? Just tell me why?"

Rafe! Hurry, please!

His free hand left the door bolt and dragged nervously across his upper lip.

"You must know, Allison. You're too beautiful. Too perfect. You—"

She heard the sound of running footsteps outside the door a bare half second before Jerry did. That instant gave her just enough time to snatch up the stool. She swung it wildly, yanking her other hand out of her pocket to protect her eyes and face as she twisted away.

She heard a grunt, followed immediately by a crash as the door kicked open. Keeping her eyes shielded, Allie dived for the door.

"Rafe!" she screamed, shoving at the solid figure before her. "Get back! He's got chemicals! He's—"

A hard hand closed around her arm and thrust her outside. Allie fell face forward, hands splayed out, at the same moment Jerry gave an enraged scream. Pain splintered through her wrists when she hit the dirt on her outflung hands. Behind her, Rafe shouted above Jerry's raging, incoherent fury.

"Drop it, Philips! Drop the damn—"

As Allie rolled to her knees, a shot rang out. She heard a crash, like the sound of a body slamming back against the supply shelves.

"Drop it!" Rafe roared again a moment later.

Just as Allie pushed herself to her feet, another shot split the night, An instant later, the world exploded.

Blinding white light seared through the processing unit as a batch of chemicals ignited. The force of the explosion threw Allie backward. She staggered into something behind her, then struggled to right herself.

"Rafe!" she screamed. "Oh, my God! Rafe!"

"What the hell—!"

Dom slapped an arm around her waist, yanking her back before she'd taken a half step toward the door.

"Rafe's in there!" she screamed, clawing at his arm. "And Jerry!"

Her nails gouged flesh. Her heels kicked shins. Dom went down, and Allie broke free of his hold. She threw her arm over her face and ran into the unit.

She found Rafe crumpled on the floor, blood pumping from a gash on his head. Sobbing, gasping for breath, she grabbed his arm and dragged his dead weight. Flames leaped all around her, licking at the walls and furniture. At her clothes, and Rafe's. Deadly fumes left a thick, clogging miasma in the air. Closing her eyes and her mouth, Allie tried not to breathe as she stumbled backward toward the open door, dragging Rafe with her.

Heat seared her face, her hands, her throat. Hissing white flames blinded her. Suddenly another shape thrust in beside her. Dom grabbed Rafe's leg and yanked. Moments later, the three of them fell out the door in a heap, arms and legs tangled.

Distantly Allie heard shouts. Dimly she felt hands drag at her to help her up. More figures bent to grasp Rafe and pull him away from the flames now shooting out the door. Allie gripped his vest and tugged with all her might.

"Dom!" Xola's voice was shrill with panic as she yanked at the photographer's arm. "Get up! That thing could blow sky-high any moment!"

"Jerry's in there!" Allie gasped when the group stumbled to a halt. "We've got to—"

Suddenly the entire processing center lifted off the ground. A huge boom split the night. Allie fell over Rafe's body, protecting it with her own.

Rafe drifted slowly out of the blackness around him. Sounds impinged on the dark, impenetrable fog. A siren wailed somewhere above his head. Metal rattled. Voices rose and fell, one masculine and unfamiliar, the other a deep, raw croak.

He frowned, trying to identify the speakers and the vibration under him. Pain lanced through him with the slight movement of his brow. White sparklers lit up the darkness with incandescent, agonizing brilliance.

A single desperate need emerged through the pain. He had to identify the speakers. He had to know whether that was Allie croaking so hoarsely. Fighting back a grunt of agony, he forced his eyelids up, first the right, then the left. Before the blinding light stopped spinning in front of his eyes, fingers feathered lightly on his chin.

"Rafe. Can you see me?"

He squinted in an attempt to stop the cartwheeling lights. "Allie?"

"I'm here, darling. I'm here."

If Rafe hadn't caught a glimpse of dark red hair through his narrow, squinting eyes, he would have thought the deep-throated voice belonged to Xola. He forced his eyes open wider to see if that could really be Allie rasping at him.

For the space of a heartbeat, he wasn't sure. The woman who leaned over him possessed deep wine-red hair, but it drooped in uneven lengths and its ragged tips curled in blackened crisps. Bloodshot brown eyes stared out of two huge white holes in an otherwise grimy face. Most of her left eyebrow had been singed off, and something he knew immediately had to be blood had smeared across one cheek.

Panic gripped him. He reached out, ignoring the sharp prick and tug of a rubber IV tube. His hand closed around her upper arm, drawing her closer.

"Are you all right?"

"I'm fine." She smoothed his hair back from his forehead. "It's you we're worried about. Jerry... Jerry slashed you with the glass jar, and threw chemicals..."

She stopped, swallowing hard. Rafe's swirling senses had cleared enough for him to grasp the meaning of her stumbling words. He wiped his tongue across cracked lips.

"Guess I'll have to get you to spread a little paint on me to cover up the dents and scars, like we did on those carousel horses."

Allie stared at him blankly for a few seconds, then gave a hiccuping sob of relief and laughter. "I'll have to spread it on both of us, although I'm not sure even Fortune Cosmetics's miracle products can repair all this damage."

Rafe took a curling crisp of hair between his thumb and forefinger. A small, painful smile lifted his mouth, but his eyes were dead serious.

"You don't need any wonder paints, sweetheart. You're the most beautiful thing I've ever seen in my life."

Hot tears splashed down Allie's cheeks. She swiped them away with the back of one hand. At that moment, she felt more beautiful than she'd ever felt before.

Thrusting out an arm to steady herself against the rock of the ambulance as it swerved around a corner, she crouched beside Rafe's stretcher and whispered promises of long, slow massages, endless nights spent spreading paint and various other materials on each other, and no morning runs for the next week or two, at least.

Fourteen

When Rafe awoke for the second time, dawn edged the curtains drawn across a pair of tall windows. Blinking, he swiped his tongue around a dry mouth.

His first conscious thought was of Allie. She'd been here with him last night. For a while. Until a green-coated doctor had ushered her out with the admonition that she needed sleep and recuperation as much as his patient.

As Rafe's mind cleared, vivid images of the events leading to the appearance of the doctor came swamping back. He remembered his pounding run across the courtyard, a fleeting glimpse of Allie's terrified face as he yanked open the door and she dived at him, trying to shove him back outside. His muscles tensed as he recalled flinging her to safety, then spinning to face the man who'd threatened her.

At that point, all hell had broken loose.

He remembered a spray of orange liquid arcing toward him. A burning sensation on his neck and forearm and face. Eyes watering from the acrid fumes. A shouted warning when Philips had smashed the jar on the edge of the table and came at him with the jagged edge. The first shot had gone into the intern's shoulder, as Rafe had intended. He'd staggered back against some shelves, then leaped forward again. The second shot had been meant to shatter his upraised arm. Rafe was sure he'd heard the sickening crunch of bone shattering at the same instant the bullet plowed into the cabinet behind Philips and ignited the chemicals.

He could remember only fragments after that. An ambulance ride. Allie's smoke-blackened face smiling down at him. Rafe lay still, letting the horror of the night recede as visions of Allie filled his mind. Even grimy and singed, she glowed with an inner beauty that made Rafe ache.

Gradually the sounds of the hospital began to impinge on his consciousness. A cart creaked along tiled hallways. Two people walked by, speaking low. The place was stirring, Rafe realized. It was time to pull himself together before Allie returned.

He pushed himself up, grimacing at the dull throb in his temple. The wash of cool air against his backside did more to stir him to action than anything else could have. Hospital gowns, Rafe decided as he slid his bare buns off the bed, were designed to get men up on their feet and out of the place as quickly as possible.

Grasping the IV hooked to his arm, he made it to the washroom. A flick of the light switch confirmed what Allie had hinted at last night. He'd soon have another set of scars to add to his collection. The chemical Philips had thrown at him had burned raw splotches on his neck and chest. Lifting a corner of the bandage taped across his forehead, Rafe grimaced at the gash carved by the broken glass jar. It started high up on his left temple, nicked the tip of his eyebrow and curved back to his cheek. Someone had sutured it. Very neatly.

Rafe taped the bandage back in place and twisted the tap. As he splashed cold water on those parts of his face that weren't bandaged, it occurred to him that his added decorations didn't particularly concern him. The most pressing items on his agenda at the moment were securing a decent set of pajama bottoms and scrounging a toothbrush from a nurse so that he could kiss Allie the moment she walked in the door.

She arrived while Rafe was pulling up the pajama bottoms with assistance from a nurse. He felt another waft of cool air on his bare backside and yanked the green cotton bottoms up around his hips. Fumbling with the knotted cord, he turned.

The moment he saw Allie, he froze.

The woman who strode into his hospital room wasn't the same one who'd leaned over him in the ambulance. She'd cropped her hair in a short pixie style. Her cheeks glowed with a blush of delicate color. Deep, copper-tinted wine glazed the full, sensual mouth that had pleasured Rafe in ways he didn't dare think about with the nurse standing so close.

"Here, let me help you."

She nudged the smiling nurse aside and took hold of the tangled strings. He stared down at the top of her newly shorn head as her nimble fingers yanked at the cord, looping it into an elaborate bow.

"Have I mentioned before that I think you have great buns?" Allie asked softly, her breath a warm wash against his bare chest.

The nurse chuckled and sailed out of the room with the tart observation that her patient was in competent hands. She nodded to the distinguished-looking gentleman with the shock of thick, white hair, who tucked his hands behind his back and discreetly studied the ceiling.

Rafe recorded their reactions only peripherally. His whole being was centered on the woman standing before him.

"No," he replied, smiling lopsidedly down at her. "You haven't."

"Well, I do. Good thing, since they're about the only part of you I'll be able to touch for a while."

Rafe curled a hand under her chin and tilted her face to his. "I think we might be able to find a couple of touchable square inches."

Allie's whole body quivered with the need to rise up on tiptoe and brand him with the force of her love.

"Later," she promised in a husky whisper. "Later, we'll find every touchable spot."

His fingers tightened on her chin, and the leap of searing hunger in his eyes told her that later would come soon. Very soon. Suppressing a shiver of urgent anticipation, she slipped free of his hold and turned to introduce the man waiting patiently by the foot of the hospital bed.

"This is Sterling Foster, Rafe. He's Fortune Cosmetics's senior attorney and one of our most trusted friends. He was in Dallas when I called my family to tell them about the explosion last night, and managed to beat everyone here."

"Everyone?"

Foster stepped forward, his hand outstretched. "Allie's sister is flying their father and mother to Santa Fe, Mr. Stone. I was closer, and came immediately."

Rafe took the man's hand and his measure. Foster's firm grip and broad shoulders suggested a man who might have seen a few fights outside as well as inside a courtroom. His years sat as well on him as his tailored suit, Rafe decided.

"I got most of the details of what happened from Allie," the attorney said quietly. "But there are still some unanswered questions that concern me."

"You and me both," Rafe replied. "But I'm still hazy on exactly what went down last night. Allie had better fill me in on the details, too."

Perching on the edge of the bed, she gave a thorough account of the frightening events.

"They recovered Jerry's body last night," she finished, twisting her hands in her lap. "His parents are flying out later today."

"He didn't give you any reason for his actions?" Rafe asked, frowning.

"None, except to say I was too perfect." She shuddered. "Too...too beautiful."

Rafe fought the sudden, murderous rage that spiked through him. Later, he might feel a twinge of sorrow at the intern's death. Right now, though, he couldn't quite forgive him for the terror and danger he'd put Allie through, or for the shadows that darkened her eyes.

"What else?" he asked.

She shook her head. "Nothing. He just kept saying that he had to hurt me."

"Maybe that fax will explain...."

"What fax?" the lawyer asked sharply.

"Here, I've got it in my purse."

Allie dug out a folded sheet and handed it to Rafe. He scanned the brief entries, his frown deepening.

"Two drug busts, one as a juvenile for selling and one last year for possession. I'm surprised the university administration let him stay in school after the last one."

"Maybe they didn't know about them," Allie suggested hesitantly. "Records are easy to suppress in some states."

Rafe wanted desperately to banish her last, lingering traces of fear. But his every instinct told him there was more behind Philips' calls than a sick obsession. Curling his fist around the fax, he met Sterling Foster's piercing blue eyes.

"It doesn't feel right."

"If you'll permit me?"

The attorney took the crumpled sheet. His unlined face remained impassive as he studied the sketchy information it contained.

"My aunt Rebecca has hired a private investigator to look into the accident that killed Kate," Allie put in slowly. "He's expanded his investigation to include the explosion at the lab. Between his contacts and yours, perhaps we can discover what drove Jerry Philips."

"We will, sweetheart." Rafe's promise was flat and hard. "We will."

Foster's eyes narrowed for a moment, then he folded the fax into neat quarters and tucked it in his suit pocket. "If you two will excuse me, I'll go make a few calls." He held out his hand once more. "You'll hear this many times in the next few days, I'm sure, but let me say it first. Thank you."

Rafe's gaze slid to Allie. "I'm the one giving thanks."

"That's going to make certain people extremely happy," the lawyer murmured obscurely as he turned to leave.

Rafe let him go. He'd get together with Foster and Jake Fortune later to decide where they went from here. Right now, his most pressing concern was Allie. Driven by a need to banish the shadows from her eyes once and for all, he tilted her face to his.

"You know," he mused, "Philips had it wrong. You're beautiful, but not perfect. Not by a long shot."

She blinked in surprise. "Is that so?"

"'Fraid so."

One dark red brow arched. "Would you care to enlighten me about those areas I'm deficient in? Just for future reference, you understand."

Rafe brushed the pad of his thumb across that wineglazed mouth. "Well, you have a tendency to rewrite rules when they inconvenience you."

"True."

"You can be hardheaded about certain things, like leaving a perfectly good bed to chug through the dawn."

"I suppose I could be a little more flexible about my schedule," she admitted grudgingly, flicking her tongue against the tip of his thumb. "No sense leaving a perfectly good bed...if there's a reason not to."

He smiled down at her. "I could give you a reason."

Allie's heart skipped several beats. She waited, willing him to say the words she saw in his eyes, felt in the stroke of his thumb against her lip.

"I love you, Allie. Seriously."

Her smile unfolded in a joyous sigh. Wrapping her arms around his bare waist, she rose on tiptoe.

"I love you, too, my darling. I *very* seriously love you."

She closed her eyes, savoring the kiss. It was gentle, because of his injuries, and warm, and so achingly wonderful Allie could have lost herself in his touch for the rest of her life. Unfortunately, an angry voice sounded outside the door just moments later.

"No, dammit, I'm not coming back during visiting hours. I've got work to do."

A moment later, the door thumped back against the wall and Dom strode in. The fluorescent lighting gleamed on his bald head. Like Allie, he'd lost his hair and an eyebrow to the singeing flames. Unlike Allie, he hadn't penciled the eyebrow in.

Xola followed at a more leisurely pace, smiling a hello while the photographer sputtered in exasperation.

"Where do these people get off? It's after ten, New York time. You okay, Stone?"

"I'm getting there." Rafe rose and held out his hand. "Allie tells me you helped drag me out of the processing center last night. Thanks."

Gray eyes met blue, and then Dom took the proffered hand in a firm grip. "Yeah, well, you're welcome. I'm just sorry the shot of Allie I was going to make into a portrait for your wedding present went up in flames."

Over his shining head, Rafe's eyes snagged Allie's. "Wedding present?"

She smiled. "Wedding present."

"You two can talk about it later," Dom exclaimed impatiently. "Right now, Allie needs to get to work. I've got backups of everything but yesterday's museum sequence. If we hump, we can reshoot it today. A little creative lighting, and no one will know she's just been scalped. Come on, Allie, let's move it."

"Hold it, Avendez."

Dom swung around. "What?"

"I need to get a few things straight with Allie before she goes anywhere."

The photographer swiped a hand over his gleaming skull. "Oh, for Pete's sake. You're not still playing watchdog? Your job's over, isn't it?"

"No, it's not," Rafe drawled, his eyes on Allie's face.

"It's not?" she asked breathlessly.

"No, sweetheart," he replied, brushing a knuckle down her cheek. "It's just beginning."

With a rich, velvety chuckle, Xola looped an arm around Dom's neck. "Why don't we wait outside? I think they want to be alone."

The photographer shot her a startled glance. For once he was silent as he was steered out of the room.

"About this business of guarding my person . . . ?" she prompted when the door had swished shut.

"I thought we'd better establish a few of the ground rules," Rafe explained, smiling down at her in a way that made Allie melt. "Something tells me the job is going to last forever."

Epilogue

"Dammit, Sterling, I don't like being dead!"

A weary smile edged the attorney's face. He'd flown all night to get back to Minneapolis after leaving Allie and her bodyguard, knowing his partner would want a first-hand report. He watched her now as she paced the apartment he'd rented for her under an assumed name, noting the flush of anger on her high cheekbones and the delicate quiver of her aquiline nose. Any one of Kate Fortune's children and grandchildren would recognize the danger signs immediately and keep a respectable distance. To Sterling, who'd been her friend for longer than he'd been her attorney, the humming vitality that radiated from her slight body was as fascinating as it was faintly alarming.

She took another turn of the room, ignoring its panoramic view of sparkling blue lakes tucked among the greenery of Minneapolis in full summer. The cane she'd needed sporadically ever since her plane went down in flames in the Amazon jungle thumped against the hardwood floors.

"May I remind you that this whole charade was your idea?" he put in mildly.

She waved an impatient hand. "I know, I know."

Foster had opposed the idea at first. For that matter, he had also opposed the idea of Kate flying her sleek little jet down to South America in search of a newly discovered species of aloe plant that would provide the secret "miracle" ingredient for her new line of cosmetics. But Kate wasn't a woman to be stopped by any person. When the charred wreckage of her plane was found deep in the Amazon jungle, he'd been as grief-stricken as any of the Fortunes.

He wasn't a man given to emotion, but those long, dark nights after Kate's funeral were the bleakest of his life. He still hadn't quite come to grips with the emptiness her death had left in his heart when the confounded woman had knocked on the door to his home one night and limped in as bold as you please, almost giving him a coronary!

As indomitable as ever, Kate had fought off the attacker who'd hidden in her plane. The struggle had sent the craft careening into the jungle canopy. Kate had been thrown clear just before the jet exploded in a ball of fire. Nursed by natives who'd taken her to their remote villages, she'd slowly recovered from the multiple injuries she'd sustained. Then she'd returned to Minneapolis and to the one man she said she trusted.

Sterling wasn't quite ready to admit, even to himself, that he was coming to want more than trust from this remarkable woman. He'd known Kate for four decades, as a friend and a client. The idea of altering that comfortable, well-established relationship made him almost as nervous as Kate's absolute determination to flush out the person who hired her attacker. It had been her idea to remain dead, and now the vibrant, independent woman was caught in her own trap.

"I should have gone out to New Mexico," she muttered irritably. "I need to see for myself that Allie's all right."

"She's fine."

"I also want to check out this Rafe Stone."

"He's a good man. A strong one, from what I could ascertain during the brief time I spent with him."

"He'd better be," Kate replied, her aristocratic features softening. "Allie's my granddaughter, after all."

Foster hesitated, reluctant to add to the burden his client already carried.

"Stone isn't satisfied that he has the answers behind what drove Jerry Philips to fixate on Allie," he said slowly. "He said..."

Kate pinned him with a sharp stare. "He said what?"

"He said it doesn't feel right."

Her swift, indrawn breath stabbed through the silence. Gripping the head of her cane with both hands, she stared at him.

"Sterling . . ."

She swallowed, then forced herself to voice the awful suspicion he saw forming in her eyes.

"What if all the setbacks Fortune Cosmetics has experienced lately are related? What if they're not isolated events?"

Slowly, deliberately, she recounted the string of misfortunes that had plagued her family.

"We still don't know who hired the man who tried to kill me. Or why the Immigration Service gave Nick and Caroline so much trouble suddenly. Then there was the fire at the lab, and now, this attack on Allie." Her grip tightened on the cane until her knuckles showed white. "What if one person is behind all this?"

Although the same suspicion had begun to wrap its tentacles around his own mind, the lawyer in Sterling was moved to protest.

"We don't have any proof, anything concrete to link these events."

Kate's chin lifted. Despite her cane and the streaks of silver threading her red hair, she looked so much like the determined young businesswoman who'd hired him as Fortune Cosmetics's first corporate attorney that he blinked.

"We'll get the proof," she said, her eyes gleaming with the light of battle. "If there's a link, we'll find it!"

Foster barely suppressed a groan. When Kate got that look on her face, she was unstoppable. The next few months, he suspected, were going to prove both exciting and highly hazardous.

* * * * *

FORTUNE'S CHILDREN

continues with

STAND-IN BRIDE

by Barbara Boswell

Available in October

Here's an exciting preview....

STAND-IN BRIDE

"Julia, look at this!" Kristina Fortune tossed a magazine directly in front of Julia Chandler, her brother Michael's executive assistant.

Julia glanced at the cover. Bold letters promised IN THIS ISSUE: THE TOP TEN MOST ELIGIBLE BACHELORS IN THE U.S.A.

"It's an advance copy. The issue doesn't hit the stands until tomorrow. Turn to page 15, Julia," Kristina ordered with an eager glee that put Julia on guard. Kristina, a rising star in the advertising department, sometimes displayed enthusiasm for concepts and notions that caused headaches for everyone else.

"The predictable choices, I see," Julia remarked as she scanned the list. She was somewhat relieved; predictability seldom caused headaches. The bachelors included a former president's son, a talk-show host, a music-business mogul, a senator, an actor, a bestselling writer, a basketball player and...

"Michael Fortune!" Julia read the name aloud and gasped.

"After the magazine hits the stands tomorrow, women all over the country will be lusting after my big brother. Mike will be a genuine sex object!'' Kristina was exultant.

Julia felt an ominous stirring within her that kept growing stronger. She'd worked for Michael Fortune for fourteen months, plenty of time to know that he would absolutely hate his new status. It was the Fortune family business that was the abiding focus of Michael's life, not popularity with the opposite sex.

"What's Mike going to say?" Kristina asked, grinning.

Julia decided it would be prudent to keep her true opinion to herself. Who knew what part, if any, Kristina had played in this surefire fiasco? When it came to dealing with the Fortunes, Julia was always cautious. "This list isn't going to, um, thrill him," she hedged. To put it mildly! "He would have preferred to be named one of the top-ten most effective businessmen."

"*Business!* That's all he thinks about!" Kristina began to move about the room.

Another pacer, Julia thought with a resigned sigh. All the Fortunes she'd met possessed a boundless, vital energy. She guessed their frequent family get-togethers must be exhausting. To a quiet, retiring person such as herself even imagining the scene was daunting!

Julia studied the picture more carefully. It was a candid shot of Michael in well-worn blue jeans and white cotton polo shirt bearing the Fortune company logo. The photo showed a compellingly virile man, whose muscular body would catch the eye of any female with a pulse. The strong features of his face—the well-defined jaw and deep-set blue eyes arched by startlingly black brows, the hard sensual shape of his mouth—guaranteed him a second glance from any appreciative male-watchers.

And even reluctant ones. Julia was well aware of her boss's masculine good looks, though she had never—nor would she ever!—let him know that she considered him attractive.

She remembered her first meeting with Michael Fortune, on the day he'd hired her fourteen months ago. The sight of him had had an unsettling physical effect on her. For the first weeks of her employment, his presence had sent a rush of adrenaline surging through her. Her heart would race and her skin would feel flushed. She was acutely aware of his every gesture, his every move.

Luckily, she'd been able to hide her attraction from everyone. Julia wasn't about to risk her job by indulging in a silly and hopeless infatuation with her boss.

An infatuation with Michael would've been as stupid as it was futile, for she knew he viewed her as something akin to office equipment. She was useful and efficient, like a fax machine, and more reliable than their copier, which was forever breaking down. His attitude toward her hardly fueled romantic fantasies, and soon Julia gratefully pronounced herself free of any.

Kristina said, "Just think—"

Michael Fortune walked through the door and finished "—of the trouble it could cause! What are you up to now, Kristina?"

"Actually, Julia and I were drooling over the hunks in this magazine." Laughing, Kristina thrust the copy into his hands.

Michael glanced at Julia, and saw her cheeks color. He felt a stirring of sympathy for her. Clearly Kristina had incorporated poor Julia into her silliness.

He instantly exonerated his assistant, because he simply couldn't imagine Julia Chandler drooling over pictures of Kristina's "hunks."

Julia was always proper, circumspect and competent, qualities he especially valued because they'd been sorely lacking in the parade of assistants who had preceded her. He still held grim memories of the time before Julia.

He'd had to endure all those snide remarks and jokes about the "revolving door" on his assistant's office. There was gossip that he was impossible to work for and would never be able to keep an assistant longer than a few months.

It had been a considerable relief when Julia had arrived and put an end to the parade.

His eyes narrowed as he continued his perusal of Julia. She wore a simple gray suit and her hair was tied back. She had a smooth, ivory complexion that contrasted nicely with the darker color of her nut brown hair. And though Julia wasn't beautiful in the classic sense, her high cheekbones, firm little chin and large gray eyes held an appeal all their own.

Not to him of course, Michael was quick to assure himself. He was not interested in pursuing a relationship with the best and longest-lasting assistant he'd ever had. He wasn't interested in pursuing a relationship with any woman that extended beyond short-term, safe sex with absolutely no strings attached. His work was the primary force in his life and he couldn't imagine anyone taking precedence over it.

"Go on, look at the magazine, Mike," Kristina ordered.

Michael frowned. "Why would I want to look at the well-oiled Neanderthals you've been drooling over?"

"Neanderthals, huh?" Kristina snickered. "Oh, I think you'll be very interested in seeing these guys, Mike. One in particular."

Julia tensed. It was like watching someone about to step in front of a speeding bus. She wanted to call out a warning, but her voice seemed to be frozen in her throat. She stood stock-still, watching as Michael cast a disdainful glance at the article.

She saw him gape in disbelief as he read the list of top-ten most eligible bachelors in the U.S.A., one of whom was him!

Stories of love and life, these powerful
novels are tales that you can identify with—
romances with "something special" added in!

Fall in love with the stories of authors such
as **Nora Roberts, Diana Palmer, Ginna Gray**
and many more of your special favorites—as
well as wonderful new voices!

Special Edition brings you
entertainment for the heart!

Do you want...

Dangerously handsome heroes

Evocative, everlasting love stories

Sizzling and tantalizing sensuality

Incredibly sexy miniseries like **MAN OF THE MONTH**

Red-hot romance

Enticing entertainment that can't be beat!

You'll find all of this, and much *more* each and every month in **SILHOUETTE DESIRE**. Don't miss these unforgettable love stories by some of romance's hottest authors. Silhouette Desire—where your fantasies will always come true....

DES-GEN

Silhouette ROMANCE™

What's a single dad to do when he needs a wife
by next Thursday?

Who's a confirmed bachelor to call when he finds a
baby on his doorstep?

How does a plain Jane in love with her gorgeous boss
get him to notice her?

From classic love stories to romantic comedies to emotional heart
tuggers, **Silhouette Romance** offers six irresistible novels every
month by some of your favorite authors!
Such as…beloved bestsellers **Diana Palmer**,
Annette Broadrick, Suzanne Carey, Elizabeth August
and **Marie Ferrarella**, to name just a few—and some sure to
become favorites!

Fabulous Fathers…Bundles of Joy…Miniseries…
Months of blushing brides and convenient weddings…
Holiday celebrations… You'll find all this and much more in
Silhouette Romance—always emotional, always enjoyable,
always about love!

SR-GEN

WAYS TO *UNEXPECTEDLY* MEET MR. RIGHT:

♡ *Go out with the sexy-sounding stranger your daughter secretly set you up with through a personal ad.*

♡ *RSVP yes to a wedding invitation—soon it might be your turn to say "I do!"*

♡ *Receive a marriage proposal by mail— from a man you've never met....*

These are just a few of the unexpected ways that written communication leads to love in Silhouette Yours Truly.

Each month, look for two fast-paced, fun and flirtatious Yours Truly novels (with entertaining treats and sneak previews in the back pages) by some of your favorite authors—and some who are sure to become favorites.

YOURS TRULY™:
Love—when you least expect it!

YT-GEN